His Sunshine

Cameron Hart

Published by Cameron Hart, 2024.

This is a work of fiction. Similarities to real people, places, or events are entirely coincidental.

HIS SUNSHINE

First edition. January 16, 2024.

Copyright © 2024 Cameron Hart.

ISBN: 979-8227686428

Written by Cameron Hart.

Want a free book?

Sign up for my newsletter[1] and get your free copy of Chasing Stacy!

One look at the stunning waitress carrying the weight of the world on her shoulders, and I'm a goner. I wasn't looking for a sweet little thing with auburn hair and more baggage than I can fit on the back of my bike, but there's no going back now. She's mine. I'll prove to her I'm more than capable of handling her past and making her feel safe again.

---

1. https://dl.bookfunnel.com/7wbqvhsx8r

Connect with me!

Check out my website, cameronhart.net[2], for sneak previews on my latest projects.

Follow me on social media:

Facebook Page - facebook.com/cameronhartauthor
   Instagram - instagram.com/cameron.hart.author
   TikTok - tiktok.com/@author.cameron.hart
   Goodreads - goodreads.com/16081533.Cameron_Hart
   Bookbub - bookbub.com/authors/cameron-hart

Chapter 1

Parker

"What do you mean, he's sick?" I bark into the phone. I'm not sure what answer I'm expecting my assistant to give me, I'm just annoyed at the sudden hitch to the start of my day.

"Um...I guess he has a fever?" my nervous assistant, Todd, says. "I'm sorry Mr. Anderson. He just called in, last minute."

"And none of the other drivers are available on such short notice?" I confirm.

"I'm so sorry. I can arrange an Uber to pick you up. Or...you could take the train?" He all but squeaks that last part out.

"What's Uber?"

Todd laughs, but then quickly regains composure. "It's kind of like a taxi. There's an app, you tell the driver where to meet you and give them your destination. It's all saved in the app so they just pick you up and drop you off. It's kind of like a chauffeur service for the rest of us. I mean...uh, sorry, sir. Mr. Anderson."

I chuckle, hoping to put Todd at ease. I may have a reputation for being an asshole, but I don't want my employees to piss their pants every time I talk to them on the phone.

"Relax, Todd. I'm not a huge fan of strangers having information saved in an app about me. I think I might take the train."

"*Really?!*" He sounds like he all but fell off his chair.

"Yeah. How bad could it be?"

I can tell Todd is holding back a number of responses. "Uh, right. Well, whatever you think is best. The 5 is probably your best bet. You can grab it at the fifty-sixth street station. It'll drop you off a few blocks away from the office."

I grunt my thanks and tell him I'll be there as soon as I can.

Ten minutes later, I'm sitting on a dirty seat in an even dirtier train. It smells like stale beer and Chinese food. The floor is sticky, and I hope it's from a spilled soda. I don't want to think about the other possibilities.

I have to remind myself that I used to take public transportation all the time. I guess I've gotten a little comfortable with my padded lifestyle. I wasn't always a millionaire. Growing up it was just my mom and me. She worked her ass off and provided the best she could.

I got into Stanford on a scholarship and got my master's in computer science and business marketing. A few friends and I graduated and started our own tech company in New York. Within the first two years, we had our own patents on specialized technology used in airplanes. We landed a few big contracts with Boeing and the U.S. military, and the rest, as they say, is history. At thirty, I'm one of the most eligible bachelors in New York.

And yet, there's something missing. I didn't know what until this moment.

Her.

She's standing on the platform wearing beat-up converse and a light pink lacy dress that hugs her tiny frame and flares at the hips. She has porcelain skin, pouty lips, green eyes, and a frizz of blonde hair that's just begging me to wrap it around my fist while I sink into her from behind. The angel has this innocence and warmth about her. I want to wrap her up in my arms and let her goodness seep into my bones while I protect her from the world.

What the fuck is wrong with me?

I've never had this kind of reaction to someone before. It's not just my painfully hard cock, it's the sudden flood of foreign emotions coursing through my mind.

The train stops, and I watch with rapt attention as the gorgeous woman gets on. My little sunshine makes her way toward the back and takes the seat across from me. *Thank God.* There's no way I'm letting her out of my sight.

I try not to openly gawk at her, but it's proving to be an impossible task. Up close I can see she has no makeup on, and I love that about her. Most of the women I see around the office or at parties paint it on thick. To the point where I don't know if I'd recognize them once they took it off. Without any makeup, I can see she has a splash of freckles on her nose and cheeks. I wonder if she has freckles anywhere else. I can't wait to kiss every single one of them as she writhes underneath me and melts into my touch.

Again, what is wrong with me? These thoughts are totally inappropriate. Sunshine looks up and smiles at me. I swear my heart stops beating.

More people start shuffling onto the train, and I give up my seat to a pregnant woman, who smiles at me with gratitude. Turning slightly, I face my beautiful sunshine, bracing myself on the bar right above her seat.

She pulls a book out of her tattered backpack and flips through the pages until she finds her spot. I'm not usually one to make small talk, and if I had a book out to read the last thing I'd want is for someone to interrupt me, but I can't stop the words from tumbling out of my mouth.

"What are you reading?"

Instead of looking annoyed, she lifts her beautiful eyes from the book and locks them on mine. She blushes. Fucking blushes. And I can't get enough of her.

"*1984*. It's like my tenth time reading through it. I love dystopian novels and the different worlds they create in such vivid detail. Orwell does an amazing job of throwing the reader right into the world, no prelude or exposition, just all action from the very beginning. I mean that opening line – 'It was a bright cold day in April, and the clocks were striking thirteen.' Brilliant, right? Don't get me wrong, I love all kinds of books. I'm a sucker for Jane Austen. Cliché, I know. But who doesn't love a happily ever after?"

She stops suddenly and I miss the melody of her voice.

"God, I'm rambling. Sorry. Bad habit." She looks away as a blush creeps onto her cheeks once more.

"Don't apologize, sunshine. It's been years since I've read *1984*, but I remember liking it. I can't say that I've ever read any Jane Austen, but if you like it, I might have to pick up a few of her books. Any favorites?"

My little sunshine gets a huge smile on her face and launches into a list of Austen classics, giving me the pros and cons of each. I never want her to stop talking. Her voice washes over me and melts away the stress of my morning.

"So, *Pride and Prejudice* is a must. Then *Sense and Sensibility*?"

She nods and then giggles. God, I love that sound. I aim to make her giggle and laugh all the time. Because, yeah, now I can't imagine my life without her in it.

"What's so funny?"

"I just can't picture someone like you reading Pride and Prejudice," she giggles again.

"Someone like me?"

"Yeah, you're like a totally muscular, ridiculously attractive, obviously successful man..." Her eyes go wide and her face turns completely red when she realizes what she said. "I-I mean, just that you're...you're..."

I laugh, hoping to ease some of her embarrassment. Inside, I'm beating my chest with pride that she finds me attractive. I bend down a little closer to her. "I'm glad you like what you see, sunshine." I wink at her and straighten up.

The train stops again, and even more people pile on. I didn't think we could fit any more after the last stop. An elderly woman hobbles on and looks around for an open seat. My sunshine pops up and waves her over. She even holds on to the woman's arm and guides her to the open seat.

Then, she takes her backpack and sets it up on the shelf before standing in front of me. Unfortunately, her back is to my front, so I don't get to see her beautiful face.

I do, however, get to smell her. There's a hint of strawberries and mint, and something that's uniquely...her. What's her name?

Before I can ask, the train jolts forward, sending my little sunshine stumbling back into me. I instinctively wrap my arm around her and spread my hand over her small waist, holding her against me.

"Oh! I'm so sorry!" She exclaims.

"I'm not," I whisper into her ear.

I hear her breath catch in her throat and see the muscles in her throat move as she audibly swallows. She reaches her hand up to grip the railing, but she's so short, only her tiny fingers wrap around it. I don't let go of her. Instead, I pull her a little closer.

"I've got you. I won't let you fall." I can see her pulse racing on the side of her neck, and I long to nip at the sensitive skin there before kissing away the sting.

"Thanks." She breathes out.

We stand in comfortable silence for a few minutes while the train hurtles towards the next stop.

"So," I say. "What's your name?"

"Hailey. What's yours?"

"Parker."

"Parker." She repeats. My cock twitches, loving the way it sounds on her lips.

"Do you come here often?" I ask, grinning down at her. I can see a smile pull at her lips when she hears my cheesy pick-up line.

"As a matter of fact, I do. Monday through Saturday. I hop on the B line to the fifty-sixth street station and take the 5 to Manhattan. Usually, I make the six a.m. bus, which puts me here in time for the six twenty-five train. And..." Hailey trails off and then clears her throat. "Anyway. That's probably way more information than you ever wanted to know about my commute. It's actually probably more than I should tell a stranger on a train. Sometimes I just don't know when to stop talking."

She turns and looks at me over her shoulder with the cutest little face. Her nose is all scrunched up and she looks annoyed with herself. I bend my head toward her, close enough that I feel her breath on my lips. The urge to kiss her, touch her, feel her softness melt into my hardness runs through my veins. But I know once I start, I won't be able to stop, and I don't want to make a scene here on public transit. Those green, doe eyes look up at me, and I wonder if she feels the same pull that I do.

"I love hearing you talk. You can tell me anything, sunshine."

She knits her eyebrows together and searches my eyes for something. Sincerity, maybe? I hate whatever put that doubt in her emerald eyes.

"This...this is my stop." I don't want her to go but I don't have any way to make her stay. I reluctantly move my hand before bending down and placing a gentle kiss on her forehead. I don't know why. It just felt like the right thing to do. Like we'd been doing it for years.

"Have a good day, sunshine," I whisper into her soft skin. I pull back and see her closed eyes and flushed cheeks.

"You too, Parker." With that, she grabs her backpack and practically sprints off the train. I miss her already.

What the fuck just happened?

One thing is for sure. I'll be riding the train into work from now on.

Chapter 2

Hailey

What the hell was that?

I noticed him as soon as I stepped on the train. Dark brown hair, ice-blue eyes, chiseled jaw, soft lips, not to mention a fitted suit that accentuated what must be a gorgeous, tight, muscular body. If I were to sum him up in two words: *man candy.*

I couldn't help but get closer. I sat across from him but couldn't quite meet his gaze. I could tell he was looking at me and I wonder what he saw.

Finally, I looked up and smiled at him, but only for a second. I proceeded to take out my worn copy of *1984* with every intention of burying my face in it for the rest of the commute. But then he asked me about what I was reading.

That was his first mistake.

Everyone who knows me for literally any amount of time can tell you I don't know when to shut up. I can't help it. All my thoughts are right there on the surface and they all just sort of run together. I've gotten better at containing my flood of thoughts, but sometimes I still slip up.

He didn't seem to mind. In fact, he asked follow up questions. I mean, who is this guy?

I still feel his warm hand against my waist, holding my body against his. I swear he could hear my heart beating out of my chest the entire time he touched me. I haven't felt so safe in years. And that kiss. Even though it was just on my forehead, it was the sweetest, gentlest gesture anyone has shown me in so long. It felt natural like we did it every morning.

For once I was completely speechless. I shake my head, banishing thoughts of the beautiful stranger. Picking up my pace, I high tail it toward the exit, needing to run away from the intense encounter I just had.

Too bad I run right into Marcus. He's one of the goons my dad borrows money from on occasion.

"Well, well, fancy meeting you here, Hailey." He grips my arms to keep me from falling, but he doesn't let go. In fact, he squeezes my biceps a little too tight. I don't say anything but try to wiggle out of his grasp. No luck. "Tell your daddy we need that money." He pulls me closer to his face and I can see his bloodshot eyes and yellow teeth. I smell his rancid breath and turn my head away. "He won't like the consequences of missing another payment."

Marcus releases me with a little shove, and I stumble backward. I turn and run up the stairs, turning left as I sprint towards the bakery I work at a few blocks away. Slipping in through the back door, I rush to the bathroom and splash cold water on my face.

It's not the first time I've been cornered by Marcus. Usually, he's not as forward as he was today. In the past, he's shown up at the bakery and just ordered a muffin or something and asked about my dad. It's simply a reminder of his presence, but it's enough to get the message across.

Today was on a different level. What the fuck did my dad do this time? He's taken out small loans before, but this seems different. The stakes feel higher. Money has always been tight, but we've managed to keep afloat. Okay, so I'm the one doing a lot of the floating, but my dad's not a bad guy. He's just going through a rough patch.

I got a job at May's Bakery when I was fourteen. Technically I wasn't old enough to work yet but May knew my momma from way back in the day, and she's taken good care of me ever since Mom passed away. I "volunteered" at the bakery, but May always paid me for my time. When I turned sixteen, she made it official. Five years later, and I still love working with May. She's my rock.

The job not only helped relieve some of the financial stress at home, but it provided a way for me to escape. I love baking. It makes sense. It's part science and part feeling. There's a method and discipline, but also an art to the perfect pastry.

Plus, May is so sweet and doesn't seem to mind my rambling on about whatever is in my head at the moment. She's the only one who doesn't find me annoying. Well, other than my handsome train stranger.

Parker.

Even just thinking about him calms me down a bit. Maybe I'll see him tomorrow morning. The thought sends butterflies to my stomach, not to mention other, lower regions of my body.

God, what is wrong with me?

I shake the confusing and overwhelming thoughts of the last hour from my mind and head out to the front of the shop to start my shift.

***

I finish wiping down the counter and check the clock – five-fifteen. My shift is supposed to be seven to three, but I try to stay as long as possible. I don't really like being home. May knows I like to stay and hang out, and she doesn't mind paying me to do so. But she reminds me all the time I need a life outside of the bakery. I need to find my own joy.

Whatever that means.

I head to the train station and hop the next one heading north. I don't live in the best neighborhood. Okay, so it's made the list of top ten worst neighborhoods in New York City ever since the internet started making lists of worst neighborhoods, but, it's home. Or, at least it's been home since mom died over ten years ago.

My dad's unlucky streak of unemployment problems forced us to move out of our family home and into increasingly smaller, less legitimate forms of housing. It started with an accident on the jobsite, which lead to back surgery and a year's worth of disability checks. When those dried up, he went looking for work, but kept getting injured or laid off.

It's been awhile since he's looked for work. I guess we're doing alright with just my job for now. The place we're currently living in is cheap, and we're on a week-by-week basis. As long as we have the money turned in by Monday morning at eight, we get the place for the next week.

It's just a one-bedroom, but we make do. Dad has his TV set up in the bedroom along with his bed and recliner. The expensive recliner was a "medical necessity" after his back injury. So was the TV. He had to have something to do while recuperating, and the old TV was on its last leg. That was the first time he took out a loan.

I sleep out in the living room, but I don't mind. Usually, my dad stays in his room so I get the rest of the place to myself. The far wall is lined with my four mismatched bookshelves. Even with the multiple bookshelves, I have stacks of books all over the floor. I can't help myself. Books are the one thing I allow myself to spend money on. I even have a little reading nook set up in the corner by the window.

Taking a deep breath, I center myself before unlocking the door to our apartment. I wonder if tonight will be a good night or a bad night. It's not that Poppa is a bad man, he's just been dealt a couple of blows in life and he hasn't quite recovered yet. There are good nights when he's almost like his old self. But, if he's been drinking, it's like he's a different person altogether. The drinking started a few years ago but really ramped up this last year.

"Hey, poppa! I'm home!"

"Hales?"

"Yup, it's me. Are you hungry?"

"I am. Are you sure you're up for cooking?" He's sober. Thank God. I really need to talk to him about Marcus.

"Sure. I don't mind. Spaghetti okay?"

He agrees and I get to work.

Twenty minutes later I bring his food into his room. He's in his chair watching reruns of *CSI: Miami*. I sit on the edge of his bed with my own bowl of pasta.

"What's up, Hales. You look stressed." I twirl some pasta on my fork, trying to think of the best way to approach the topic. "You can talk to me. I know I'm not the best dad, but I'd like to think I can at least listen to your problems and try to help you if I can."

"You're a good dad!" It's my automatic response. I hate people feeling bad about themselves. Life is hard enough without that little voice of self-doubt. How am I supposed to bring up Marcus now?

"Come on, jellybean. You can talk to me."

I smile at his endearment. "I uh...I ran into Marcus on my way to the bakery this morning.

My dad's face immediately crumbles, and I regret saying anything. "What did he say?"

"Oh, just the usual. Reminded me they need their money."

"I'm so sorry, Hales. I'm working on it. I'll have enough for the next payment soon."

"What happened, dad? I thought I told you to come to me first if you needed money."

"I hate asking you for more. It's *embarrassing* to not be able to provide for my goddamn daughter," he growls. I tense up beside him. He's usually only this short when he's been drinking. Dad takes a deep breath. "I'm sorry, Hailey. I didn't mean to snap at you. I thought I had a sure thing. a friend of a friend who had a tip about someone throwing a fight. A boxing match. I was going to make us half a million. More than enough to live off of. Even send you to college."

"Poppa..."

"I know, I know. It didn't work out. But I'm fixing it, I promise."

Neither one of us says anything as the TV drones on in the background. I pick at my food, no longer hungry. Finally, I ask, "How much money, dad?"

"It doesn't matter."

"You know it does."

He sighs. "A hundred thousand."

I don't respond. I can't respond. It might not be a lot to some people, but it might as well be a million dollars to us. Hot tears prick the corners of my eyes and I swallow a lump in my throat. *What the hell are we going to do?*

"I know I let you down. I'll make it up to you. I just need some time. If you see Marcus again, just give him five hundred. That'll be enough for now."

I want to say, *"Five hundred is about four hundred more than we have,"* but I just nod instead. I'll figure it out. It wouldn't be the first time I played Russian roulette with the bills. It's easier to deal with bill collectors than Marcus.

"Okay, dad. I'll figure it out." He doesn't say anything else, so I just collect our plates and head back out to the kitchen.

After cleaning up, I take my book out of my backpack and curl up in my reading corner. I can't seem to get caught up in the world George Orwell created, however. My mind keeps wandering back to Parker. I wonder what his evenings look like. I'm sure they are nothing like mine. I wonder for the hundredth time today if I'll see him on the bus tomorrow.

I drift off with thoughts of those liquid blue eyes and the way his soft lips felt pressed against my forehead.

Chapter 3

Parker

It's official. I'm obsessed.

I can't stop thinking about Hailey. I can't believe I didn't get her number or her last name. At least with a full name I could try and look her up. I have connections. And money.

Like I said. Obsessed.

I've resigned to the fact that I'll have to wait to see her until morning. It's been a long time since I've had to wait for anything, and I don't like it.

My day goes by excruciatingly slow, filled with a bunch of things that aren't nearly as important as obsessing over my sunshine. Board meetings, signing waivers, listening in on conference calls...I honestly don't remember a single conversation I've had today except for my exchange with Hailey. In fact, right in the middle of a meeting I emailed my assistant and told him to go find *Pride and Prejudice* and *Sense and Sensibility*.

I was able to arrange a ride home with a different driver, right after calling the company to let them know I won't be needing their services in the mornings for the foreseeable future. Once I get Hailey to move in with me, we'll both use the driver. Until then, I'll be with her on the bus in the mornings.

Again. Obsessed.

But I don't feel weird about it. I feel good. Really good. It feels right.

I suppose I've always been this way. Once I make a decision, I go all in. When I decided I wanted to go to college, I set my sights on the master's program at Stanford and studied my ass off to make it happen. Starting the company was the same way – even if it meant spending all the money I had at the time and moving across the country.

Not that Hailey is a prize to be won or a challenge to conquer. She's everything, and she needs to know I'm all in. I'll lay my kingdom down at her feet for just one more smile from her soft, sweet lips.

Thinking about kissing my angel has my dick hardening to the point of pain. I groan and shift from where I'm sitting on my couch. Never, in all my years, have I reacted this way to someone. I adjust myself in my pants, trying to resist the urge to jack off, but it's pointless.

Before I know it, my cock is in my hand and I'm pumping up and down, spreading precum all over my ten inches. I picture kissing her slender neck and licking my way down to her chest before sucking on her perfect tits. In my mind, she's throwing her head back and moaning as I fingerfuck her with one hand and pinch her nipples with the other. I wonder what she looks like when she comes.

I imagine bending her over this couch and sinking into her juicy pussy as she screams my name. I thrust into her again and again, wrapping her blonde hair around my fist to pull her head up so I can kiss and bite her neck while I continue to fuck her hard. Hailey looks back at me over her shoulder like she did this morning on the train, only this time there's heated desire in her gaze.

She squeezes her eyes shut and parts her lips as she comes hard, shattering in my arms. Picturing her in pure ecstasy sends me over the edge and I grunt my release as I come harder than I have in a long time. Maybe ever. Rope after rope of cum spurts over my abs. I'm glad I'm already sitting on the couch otherwise I might just fall over from the force of it all.

Fuck.

I clean up and head to bed, more determined than ever to make Hailey mine.

***

I look very out of place here at the train station, but I don't give a fuck. I'd look like a fool every day for the rest of my life if it meant I had a chance to see my sunshine. I know I've only been here for a few minutes, but I swear each second feels like a fucking year.

Finally, I see Hailey's golden hair, which is piled on top of her head in a messy bun, shining like the sun just for me. She's wearing the same Converse shoes, paired with some galaxy leggings that make me smile, as well as a loose sweater that hangs off one shoulder. Hailey is carrying a gigantic cup of coffee, which makes me smile even more. The cup looks extra large in her small, delicate hands.

My sunshine likes her caffeine. Noted.

I continue to watch her as she takes the last couple of stairs down to the platform. She misses the last step, and before I can get to her, she's crashing to the ground. Coffee goes everywhere, earning her a few dirty looks from the people walking around her. I growl at everyone near my sunshine, not caring that it makes me seem crazy. I've been feeling pretty damn crazy ever since I met Hailey twenty-four hours ago.

"Fucking goddamnit!" I hear her swear. The tightness in my chest loosens ever so slightly at her muttered words. She must not be hurt too bad if she has the energy to swear like a sailor. I hate that she fell, but I love her dirty mouth.

Instead of lingering on the idea of Hailey's dirty mouth, I stand in front of her and offer my hand to help her up. "You okay, sunshine? You took quite a spill."

"Parker! Shit. I was looking forward to seeing you, but this is not exactly my best moment. I mean, not that I was like, thinking about you all night or whatever. I just meant because I saw you yesterday..." she clears her throat as a slight blush spreads across her perfect cheeks. "Anyway. I'm fine. Just my pride."

She takes my hand and I pull her up with a little too much force, which sends her stumbling right into my chest. She's so small, I'll have to remember to be gentle with her. "I'm glad you're not hurt," I say, smiling down at her before brushing my lips to the shell of her ear. "And for the record, I *did* think about you all night."

I pull back to see her bite her bottom lip in an attempt to hide her smile. It's so damn cute. I want to bite her lip. My cock is interested in that as well.

I clear my throat, trying to disperse of my filthy thoughts. I'm guessing it's generally frowned upon to have an erection on public transit. "Sorry about your coffee. Do you usually get a drink in the mornings?"

"Ugh, I'm so sad about that! I hardly ever buy coffee, but I had a full punch card, so it was free today. I had been working on the thing for five months!" Hailey says exasperatedly while throwing her arms up in defeat. "Oh well. I really shouldn't complain since I get free coffee at work. It's just the brewed stuff but it gets the job done. Sometimes a girl just wants a caramel latte with extra whipped cream, ya know?"

I can't help but grin through her whole monologue. She really is something else. I love hearing her voice and following her train of thought. Caramel latte with extra whipped cream. Another detail about her I'll cherish.

"Where do you work, sunshine?"

"May's Bakery. I've been there since I was fourt...sixteen. First and only job. I wouldn't want to be anywhere else." She smiles, and just like yesterday, it stops my heart.

I didn't miss the part where she almost said she started working when she was fourteen. But that seems like a conversation for another time. "Sounds like you really love what you do."

"Oh my gosh, yes. I love baking. May even lets me come up with my own pastries sometimes."

The train pulls into the station, and I place my hand on the small of Hailey's back to guide her toward the door. I can't help the wicked grin that spreads across my face when she shivers at my touch.

Once seated, I assume my position standing in front of her, like I did yesterday. I know the train is going to get crowded, so I might as well stand up now. Sunshine looks up at me and then away like she's not sure what to do next.

Good thing I have plenty of conversation topics.

"So, you work at the bakery making amazing pastries and drinking a ton of coffee. What do you do in your free time?"

"I didn't say my pastries were amazing. I've had quite a few duds. One time, I was going for a savory kind of pastry with bacon and cheese, but I didn't know much about cheeses at the time. Or how to cook bacon. Long story short, I used blue cheese in the pastry and the whole kitchen smelled like a dirty foot. Plus, the bacon bits pretty much turned into charcoal pieces even though the dough was undercooked. It wasn't my proudest moment." She scrunches up her nose as if she's remembering the smell. I log the look on her face as her third most adorable look, right behind her shy blush and, of course, her glittering smile.

"I would have tried one," I say.

She looks at me incredulously. "Uh, no. I wouldn't have let you. Trust me, they were not fit for human consumption. But, anyway. You asked what I do in my free time?" I nod, eager for more of her words. "Not much, to be honest. You already know I like to read. Other than that, I work pretty long shifts at the bakery six days a week. Not that I'm complaining. It's my favorite place to be. I'd work Sundays too if May let me, but she says I need to go out and find my joy, whatever that means. I guess I'm pretty boring." She shrugs.

"I don't think anything about you is boring, sunshine." I'm rewarded with a smile and a blush. Favorite looks one and two at the same time.

"Why do you call me sunshine?"

"That's what you are. My little ray of sunshine. I knew it when I first saw you standing on the platform yesterday. Your golden hair and brilliant smile lit up the entire train."

I was hoping for another smile, but she looks down at her hands instead. I think I embarrassed her. Does no one say nice things to my girl? I aim to change that ASAP. However, I don't want her uncomfortable around me so I change the subject.

"Work and home, huh? Do you have a roommate?" It's a little intrusive right off the bat, but I can't help it. I want to know every detail of her life, and I want to know *now*.

"I live with my dad. He's sort of...between jobs at the moment."

By now I'm used to her long-winded answers, but she doesn't elaborate. "I'm sorry to hear that, Hailey. That must be a lot of pressure to take on everything." She simply nods at my response. I hate this. I hate her being quiet.

"Um, so, anyway...what do you do? I've just been blabbing away over here. I never even got a chance to ask you anything yesterday."

"You're not blabbing, you're just talking. I love hearing you talk, don't ever doubt that." She looks skeptical but accepts my words. "But, since you asked, I own a tech company with some friends I graduated college with. Atlas Technology. We've been in business for about five years."

"Oh wow! That's amazing. Your parents must be so proud of you." She's beaming up at me and I feel like the fucking king of the world.

"It's just my mom and me, but yeah. She's always been supportive of everything I do."

"Wait, why are you taking the train? I mean, obviously, it's fine. It's open to the public, what with it being *public transportation* and all. But don't you have a helicopter or something that could take you where you want to go?" Her green eyes turn from curious to embarrassed in a matter of seconds. "Wow. That sounds so judgmental of me. Never mind. Forget I asked that." She looks down at her hands again.

I chuckle and bring my forefinger under her chin to tilt her face up toward me. "You can ask me anything, sunshine. No, I don't have a helicopter, but I usually have a driver. Yesterday he was sick, which is why I took the train. And today... Well, today I just wanted to see you again." I smile, hoping I didn't just blow it and scare her off. If she only knew how serious I was about her.

"Oh." I grin when I see her blush return, as well as a soft smile.

"Can I get your number?" I ask, taking another risk.

"I, uh, this is my stop actually. Sorry. I have to go."

Shit. Too much too soon.

Way to go, asshole.

I step back to give her space to stand up, but before she can get away, I reach for her hips and pull her into me. I place a kiss on her forehead like I did yesterday.

"Have a good day, sunshine," I murmur before pulling back and smiling down at her. She bites her lip and nods before taking off.

I let her get away - for now. I know where she works so I have a way to see her again. It's the only way I can let her get on with her day, even though it takes all of my self-restraint not to throw her over my shoulder and carry her off to my penthouse.

Soon, my little sunshine.

Chapter 5

Hailey

I'm still floating as I make my way to May's. Parker seemed to actually like talking to me. *Me!* He even said so himself.

"I love hearing you talk, don't ever doubt that."

God. *Swoon.*

I walk in the bakery and am greeted by a smiling May. "Good morning, dear. What put that goofy grin on your face?"

So much for being subtle. "Just seeing you, of course," I respond.

"Oh, child. That's not the smile you usually give me. No, that smile can only mean one thing." I quirk an eyebrow at her. "Did you meet someone, dear?"

"What? No, of course not!" I say all too quickly.

"Mmhm." May gives me a knowing look. "I won't press you for information, but I want you to know you deserve to be happy. You've had a lot of darkness in your life and a lot of responsibility. Don't be afraid to let good things in and let someone take care of you for once."

"Yes, momma bear," I roll my eyes at her. It's not often May gives me life advice, but she knows I pay attention when she does. Even if I have to lighten the mood with an eye roll or a joke.

"Enough of that. These pastries aren't going to bake themselves."

And with that, we fall into our morning routine. We switch off prepping and pulling things out of the oven while also waiting on customers. I'm in the middle of making cookies when May comes back to the kitchen with a grin on her face.

"You, my dear, have a very handsome visitor. Was he the one who put that smile on your face this morning?" I blush but don't deny it. "Well, if he's at all responsible for your happiness, then I approve. Now don't keep him waiting!" She swats me with a rag as I run up to the counter.

"Hi," I say a little too enthusiastically. Parker breaks out into a gorgeous smile, showing me his perfect teeth.

Could this guy be any more handsome?

"Hey, sunshine. I couldn't stop thinking about you all morning, so I decided to come visit."

"Awesome!" I practically shout. I cringe at my dorkiness and try to reign in my excitement. "I mean of course. We're always glad to have new customers. What can I get for you?"

He just grins at me, like he knows exactly why I'm so flustered. "Did you make any of these pastries?"

I nod. "I did the chocolate hazelnut turnovers, maple pecan scones, and Dutch letters," I say, proudly. I don't have much in my life I'm confident about, but I know my baked goods are delicious.

"What's a Dutch letter?"

"Oh my gosh, you've never had one? You have to try it. The dough is so flakey and buttery. It takes forever to get the right consistency. After making the dough, you have to fold it a bunch of times to get tiny air pockets. And then you let it rest for a while and fold it again. Then, repeat the process a few more times. It's *so* worth it. They are filled with a sweet almond paste that compliments the savory, buttery dough. Seriously, I'm not taking no for an answer. Here, I'll even give you a free sample."

I break off a piece of one of the letters in the case and hand it to him. Parker reaches out, only instead of taking the pastry, he gently grabs my wrist and brings it closer to his mouth. Then he takes a bite with the pastry still in my hand. His eyes never leave mine. Why is that so hot?

"Oh my *God*, sunshine. You made this? It's incredible."

"Told you!"

"That you did." He smiles and we just stare at each other for God knows how long. Then his cell phone rings and the moment is broken. He looks at it and frowns. "Sorry. The real world awaits. I'll take two

Dutch letters. Actually, better make it three. I'm officially addicted. And a cup of coffee, to go."

He answers his phone while I gather the pastries and pour him a cup of coffee. In a bold move, I write my number on his cup. Parker hangs up and pays for his coffee and Dutch letters.

"What's this, sunshine?"

"Um..." My cheeks are on fire. "My number..."

He flashes me a devious smile and...my panties are wet. Like, embarrassingly so. That's new. He takes out his phone and immediately enters my info. A few seconds later I feel my phone buzz in my pocket.

"You beat me to the punch. I was going to leave you my number." Parker winks and I can't help but smile at him and lean closer. He's like a freaking magnet and I can't get enough of his smile, his touch, his words.

I hold my breath as Parker leans in too. He hooks his finger under my chin and brushes his lips against mine. It's not a kiss, just a whisper of what's to come. Just enough to leave me wanting so much more. He pulls back slightly and kisses my forehead before resting his forehead there as well.

"Soon, my little sunshine." Parker stands up and walks toward the door, and I'm left staring after him in a daze. He looks over his shoulder when he gets to the door, giving me a wink and a wicked grin.

He's gone for all of thirty seconds before my phone buzzes in my pocket.

Parker: Thank you for making my day, sunshine.

My tummy does a flip and I can't help the stupid happy grin that spreads all over my face.

"Oh, you got it bad," May says with a chuckle.

"What? No, it's not...we just met."

"Still. You got it bad. I don't blame you. He is one fine piece of man meat."

"Oh my *God*, May!"

"I may be old, but I ain't dead, honey," May says with a wink.

I can't help the smirk that spreads across my lips. "I prefer to think of him as man candy."

"Well whatever you think of him as, he's just as crazy about you." I tilt my head down, hoping to hide my blush from her. "You deserve this, Hailey. I'm happy for you. Now go take your break and text him back, or stalk him on Facebook, or whatever you kids do these days."

I roll my eyes but can't help the giggle that slips out of my mouth.

Me: Thanks for coming to see me today

I see three bubbles pop up and know he's typing out a response. Knowing he was the first to text, and that he was waiting right by his phone for a reply makes me fall for him even more.

Parker: Of course, sunshine. I like seeing where you work.

Parker: I'm on my second Dutch letter, by the way. I'm sure I'll gain 15lbs by the end of the week. I should probably be mad at you.

Me: How can you be mad when they taste so good?

Parker: They are good, but not nearly as sweet as your lips.

Me: How would you know? You barely even kissed me!

Me: I mean it was a nice first kiss though. I've never had one.

Shit. I instantly regret the text as soon as I send it. Bubbles appear and then disappear. And then appear and disappear again. *Double shit.*

Me: Never mind. Ignore that last text.

Me: You'd think I'd have a better filter on my word vomit through texting. Apparently not.

Parker: Jesus, sweetheart. You can't say stuff like that to me.

Me: Why not?

Parker: It makes me want to storm into the bakery, throw you over my shoulder, and haul you to the nearest flat surface so I can give you all your firsts.

Oh, God. Yes, please.

Seriously, who is this guy? Why is someone so amazing interested in me? And furthermore, why can I already picture forever with him?

Parker: I'd like to talk to you all day, sunshine, but I have a meeting. Call me when you get home. Don't work too late, sweetheart.

I'm not sure how to respond to all of his care and attention. I type out a few words only to delete them a second later. Finally, I land on the super mature response of a winking smiley face emoji. *I'm suck a dork.*

The rest of the day goes by normally, though I'd be lying if I said I wasn't more than a little distracted by thoughts of Parker. It's just after five-thirty when I get home. I can already tell it's going to be a long night when I walk in the door and smell stale beer.

"Where the fuck have you been?"

"Dad, you know I work at the bakery every day except Sunday." I try to keep my tone light.

"Yeah, you don't have to rub it in."

So many responses flash through my mind, but I've learned to keep my words to myself when my dad is drunk and depressed like this. Changing the subject, I ask what he wants for dinner.

"I'd love steak and potatoes."

"We can't really afford that right now."

"I'm sure we can just this once. What's an extra twenty bucks? I'm already fucked, might as well eat some goddamn steak."

"Twenty bucks *is* a big deal when you're trying to pay off a *one-hundred-thousand-dollar* debt. Every penny counts, dad."

Shit. I shouldn't have said that. Instant regret fills me up, nearly suffocating me. Parker may appreciate my lack of filter, but no one else does.

"You watch that mouth of yours," he seethes. "I'm doing the best I can."

"Why don't you get a job then?"

Shut up. Shut up. Shut up!

My dad snarls and lunges at me, forcing me to take a step back. He's never physically hurt me, but he seems a little more unhinged tonight. "You don't know what it's like in my head, in my body." He keeps walking towards me till my back is against the wall. "Don't you ever talk to me like that again, got it?" He's inches away from me, caging me in with his large body. I nod, afraid to open my mouth and have something stupid come out. He slams his fist against the wall, inches from my head. I scream and he covers my mouth with his other hand. "Shut your goddamn mouth for once in your life." He stumbles back to his room and I'm left shaking, trying to gather my thoughts.

It's after seven by the time I serve and clean up dinner, take a shower, and settle in for the night with a book. I check my phone for the first time since coming home, and see I have a ton of missed calls and messages from Parker, each one more frantic with worry than the last.

Me: I'm so sorry, I just looked at my phone. I'm home, no need to worry.

Parker: Sunshine, thank fuck. Everything okay?

Me: It will be. Just a long night.

Parker: Do you want to talk about it?

Me: Not really.

Parker: Something with your dad? He's the one thing you won't talk about.

Me: You're pretty observant...

Parker: When it comes to you, I never miss a detail.

Me: You're a pretty smooth talker ;)

Parker: Hailey... You're avoiding the subject.

Me: Yeah, it's my dad. We kinda got in a fight. But it's really okay.

Those three pesky bubbles appear, disappear, and reappear a few times, like he's not quite sure how to respond. I really don't want to get into the details right now. I just want to forget this whole night happened and fall into the pages of a book.

Parker: Thank you for telling me, sunshine. I want every detail of your life, but I know it will take time for you to trust me. Now, tell me what you're up to right this second.

I smile as tears gather in my eyes. I can't explain it, but I feel the genuineness of his words. He really does want every detail – and considering how many details I can give on any given subject, that's saying a lot. More than that, however, Parker knew I couldn't quite handle pouring my heart out right now, so he changed subjects.

Me: I'm getting settled in my reading nook with one of my favorite books.

Parker: Reading nook? Sounds swanky.

Me: It's nothing special, but it's my little space.

Parker: Can I see?

I rearrange a few things so it looks a little more put together, then snap a picture and send it to him. It takes all of two seconds for doubt to set in. What if he thinks it's stupid? What if he thinks *I'm* stupid?

Me: Like I said, it's not much. I mean, I know it's kind of childish.

Parker: I love it. It looks safe and cozy and warm. Is that in your room?

Me: Yeah, it's in the living room.

Parker: Please don't tell me you sleep on a couch.

My heart drops to my stomach at his response. Would that be a dealbreaker for him? He has to know he's out of my league, but maybe sending him that photo made him realize just how far he'd have to fall to get to my level. I don't know what to say so I just set the phone down and open my book.

A few minutes later, I get a call from Parker. I almost don't answer, but I find I want to hear his voice, even if he's just going to brush me off. How fucked up is that?

"Hey," I answer, keeping my voice low so as not to wake my dad.

"I'm sorry, sunshine. I didn't mean to scare you off or come across as judgmental. I just want to get to know you."

"It's okay, Parker. I get it."

"It's not okay. I'm sorry I made you uncomfortable." It's been so long since someone has apologized to me that I'm not sure how to respond. Good thing Parker doesn't let me feel awkward for too long. "Talk to me, what are you thinking about?"

"Honestly?"

"Always, sunshine."

"I'm thinking that it's really sweet that you wanted to make sure I was okay."

He lets out a huge breath, almost like he'd been holding it the whole phone call. "So I didn't fuck this up?"

I laugh. "No, Parker. Thank you for calling."

He asks me about the book I'm reading and I'm all too happy to talk about that instead of my home life. We end up talking for the better part of an hour about nothing and everything. He tells me about his mom and his company. I tell him what I remember about my mom and all about working at May's. Finally, we hang up and he makes me promise to text him when I get up so we can meet at the train station.

***

I wake up with a smile on my face. Despite a terrible encounter with my father, the night ended on a good note. Parker didn't press too much, but rather helped put my mind at ease by talking to me about whatever I wanted to. He listened to me ramble on and on, but he never seemed to get lost, like a lot of people do.

In an attempt to smooth things over with my dad, I get up early and make us a nice breakfast of pancakes and eggs. I bring my dad's plate into his room but stop short when I open the door. There's a bunch of empty beer cans along with a syringe what I assume are drugs scattered on his bedside table. I don't know enough about any of that stuff to guess at what the tar-like black substance is.

My eyes dart between the drugs and my dad's limp body sprawled out on the bed. I rush over to him, dropping the plate in the process. "Dad! *Dad*, are you okay? Wake up! Wake *up*!"

He grunts and rolls over.

Thank God.

"Get the hell off of me!" He shoves me off the bed and I crash into the side table, sending pain ricocheting across my ribcage.

"Dad...what have you done?"

I'm not trying to antagonize him, but I honestly don't understand how to process what I'm seeing. How can he throw away money on drugs when I've given up so much just to keep us afloat?

My father stares down at me, his eyes dull and sunken into his face. "I'm a dead man anyway, Hailey. We both know that."

"This isn't you, dad. This isn't who you are. I can get you help. I'll find another job. We'll pay off the debts. You can go to rehab, get clean, we'll move—"

"Shut up!" he roars. I hear the slap before I feel it. I'm so shocked I don't even cry. I can't. "Fuck. If I knew that's what it would take for you to finally be quiet, I'd have done it years ago."

"This isn't you, daddy," I whisper. "Please..."

He raises his hand again, but I scramble out of the way. Dad growls and tries to grab me, but ends up falling out of bed and crashing to the floor.

"*Shit*!" he yells.

I grab my backpack and shoes and run out the door, not stopping to put my shoes on until I'm a good block away. I keep running, but eventually slow down enough to not look suspicious.

Now that the adrenaline has worn off, I'm shaky and cold. I take a few deep breaths, wincing at the sharp pain in my side. My cheek stings as well, and I reach up, wiping away a bit of blood. I'm sure I look like an absolute mess.

My phone buzzes with a text as I'm digging through my backpack for my sunglasses.

Parker: Morning, beautiful. Are you up yet?

Reading his words, knowing he's thinking about me right at this moment, calms me down in a totally unexpected way. I'm not too far off schedule from my usual day, so I decide to act as if everything is normal. I can be normal. Not that I have much a choice. I can't deal with any of this right now, so I just have to keep going through the motions.

Me: I'm almost at my bus stop. I should be at the station in 25 minutes.

Parker: I'll be anxiously waiting. Can't wait to see you.

Me: Me too.

I walk the rest of the way to the bus and try to get in the right mindset to see Parker. I don't want him to know what happened. He's the one bright spot in my life, and I can't risk scaring him off with all my drama and baggage.

Chapter 5

Parker

God, I miss her. It's crazy how painful it was to hang up last night, knowing she was sleeping on a couch in what has to be an unsafe apartment on the wrong side of town. With each story we shared, I fell more and more in love with her. She's sweet and caring and sees the good in everyone, despite the shitty hand she's been dealt. My sunshine is quirky and hilarious, but so easily embarrassed. I'll work on that. I want her to be confident in who she is.

After we ended the call, I got to work on a few things in preparation for her moving in with me. I know it may be a little premature, but I know she's going to be mine. I have to get her out of her current situation. It's my new number one priority. I just have to get her to agree to it.

I feel Hailey before I even see her. I know she's close. Turning toward the entrance to the train station, sure enough, she's walking my way. My girl is in the same ratty shoes she always wears, skinny jeans, a fitted white t-shirt that make her breasts look amazing, and a pretty, pink cardigan. She has huge sunglasses on today despite it not being all that bright out. Maybe she has a headache? When she sees me, she gives me a tentative smile.

"Hey, sunshine, you okay?" She nods. "I got you a large caramel latte with extra whipped cream. That's your favorite, right?"

I'm rewarded with a huge smile and she unexpectedly throws her arms around my neck, almost making me drop our drinks. Totally worth it. This is closer than we've ever been, and I soak up the feeling of her body pressed against mine.

"If this is the reaction I'm getting for bringing you coffee, I can't wait to see what you'll do when I buy you dinner." She's still hanging on to me and I hear a laugh, followed by a sniffle. "Hey, what's wrong?"

She pulls away and I instantly miss her warmth. "Nothing, sorry. This is just really nice of you. I needed something good this morning. Thank you."

"Are you sure everything is okay, Hailey?" She nods again right before the train stops in front of us. I reach out to pull her closer to me, but she flinches like I'm going to hit her. "I'm not going to hurt you, sweetheart," I murmur in a calming voice.

"Sorry. I'm a little jumpy."

I frown, getting more concerned by the second. "Are you sure you're alright?"

"I'm sure. I'm just being weird."

She turns and walks onto the train. I sit next to her, noticing how she still has her sunglasses on. Taking her tiny hand in mine, I squeeze gently, hoping to get her to look at me. Something is wrong. This isn't my sunshine.

"What's going on? Talk to me. I love hearing your thoughts."

She doesn't say anything for a long moment, and I try to think of some way to get her to open up to me.

"You don't have to be nice to me." She whispers, almost too quiet for me to hear.

"What? Why would you say that?"

"I just...I know I'm annoying and I talk too much and...it's okay. You can walk away. I get it."

She might as well have ripped my heart out of my chest and cut it in two. Why would she ever think that about herself? "Where is this coming from? Have I made you feel that way?"

"No, no, not you," she rushes to say. "I'm sorry. I'm not myself this morning. You're wonderful. You're always so wonderful. God, I'm fucking this all up," she mutters.

"No, Hailey, you're not doing anything wrong. Talk to me."

She shakes her head softly, then whispers, "I can't."

Fuck. It's her dad. It has to be. "Can you at least look at me?" She keeps her head down, her golden locks falling in front of her face. I don't like this. I don't know what happened, but I have a sinking feeling in my gut.

I slowly move my hand to the side of her face in an effort to not startle her. I tuck some of her hair behind her ear. She tries to turn her face away, but I see it.

"Don't," she whimpers desperately. The sound completely shatters me.

"Hailey," I say in a stern and calming voice. My rage is boiling beneath the surface, but I have to remain calm for her. "I need to take off your sunglasses, sweetheart." She shakes her head and tries to jerk away again. "Baby, please, you're killing me. I'm not going to hurt you. Please let me see your face."

She stills and I gently remove her glasses.

Fuck.

The side of her face is swollen and red and she has a small gash under her eye. She won't look at me. Tears start to form, and it fucking guts me.

"Your dad," I growl, the low, gravelly sound rattling through me. Hailey starts trembling next to me. I can feel the fear and anxiety rippling off of her small body. "It's okay, you're okay," I whisper in a much calmer tone. "You don't have to talk about it right now. I'm so sorry this happened." I pull her in my arms to hold her closer to me, but she yelps in pain and clutches her left side.

Goddamnit. What else did he do to her?

"I'm fine, I'm sorry," she says through tears. I hold her hand again, the only place I'm sure of that she's not hurt.

Resting my forehead on the top of her head, I whisper, "Are you hurt anywhere else? Your face, your ribs, anywhere else?"

She shakes her head no.

I kiss the top of her head and put an arm around her hips, careful to avoid her side. I pull her closer to me as the train barrels toward the next stop. I'm sure of two things. I'm not letting her go back there, and I'm going to seriously fuck up her dad.

Finally, I say, "Did this happen last night? Is that why it was a rough night?"

"No..."

"Sunshine, did this just happen this morning?"

More tears fall into her lap. Dammit. Why didn't she call me? I would have rescued her. I would do anything for her. I try to remind myself that we only met a few days ago. While she's my whole world, I'm not hers. Yet. Plus, I can't imagine how scared she was. That kind of fear doesn't allow for rational thought.

"I'm so sorry I wasn't there, Hailey. I won't leave you again. I'll keep you safe. I'm here now." She nods and finally leans into my chest. "Can I call May for you and get someone else to cover your shift?"

"No, I should go into work today. I can't leave her."

"Sweetheart, I don't think you should work today. You've been through a traumatic event. I need to get you to the hospital and make sure your ribs aren't broken." Just the thought of it makes me see red again.

"No! No hospitals. Please, please, no hospitals."

"Hailey..."

"Parker...I don't have insurance," she says under her breath.

"I'll cover it. For me. Please let me take you."

"I-I can't go. It's where my mom died." Hailey chokes down a sob.

Well, fuck.

"Alright," I say softly. "If you call out of work, I won't take you to a hospital."

Hailey nods and snuggles deeper into my side. I still feel little tremors in her body every so often but eventually, she relaxes in my embrace, surrendering to my care.

Chapter 6

Parker helps me off the train and we walk to his office building. He refuses to let go of my hand the entire way there. When we get inside, he leads me toward the elevator bank and hits the button for the thirty-third floor. We step into the elevator and he pulls me close, wrapping his arms around me and tucking my head under his chin.

I feel so safe and warm in the protection of his arms. I grab on to his suit jacket and pull him closer, needing his strength in this moment. Parker holds me and gently rocks me in his arms.

"I've got you, sunshine. I won't let anything bad happen to you. I've got you." He whispers.

The ding of the elevator breaks the moment. He takes my hand and we step out into the most stunning lobby I've ever seen.

Everything is clean lines and light colors. There's a little room divider that's a glass wall with water cascading down, landing in a little pond with fish and floating flowers. Green snake plants are strategically placed around the area, along with white couches. The lighting is slightly dimmed, giving everything a calm and natural vibe.

I feel way underdressed, but Parker doesn't seem to notice. He lifts my hand up and kisses my knuckles.

"Do you like it?"

"Yeah...I mean, what's not to like?"

He grins and then turns to the lady behind the front desk. She's freaking gorgeous. With long, silky brown hair and dark, piercing eyes, she seriously looks like a model. She's poured into a tight red dress that highlights her stunning body. Her flawless lipstick matches her dress. A surge of jealously floods my veins and a ridiculous thought pops into my head. *He's mine, bitch.*

"Martha, this is Hailey. Hailey, my secretary, Martha."

Martha gives me the stink eye, and I don't blame her. I literally look like something the cat dragged in. She turns her face toward Parker and gives him a seductive smile, leaning forward on the desk so her boobs are practically falling out of her dress. Parker doesn't give her a second glance as he ushers me into his office.

"She's beautiful," I say once we're inside.

He stops and turns to look at me. Gently cupping my face with one hand and removing my sunglasses with the other, Parker leans down so we're staring at each other. His eyes flit all around my face like he's not sure where exactly to look. He finally lands on my eyes.

"Sunshine, *you* are beautiful. Gorgeous. Flawless. There isn't a word to describe you. You're everything to me." He rests his forehead on mine as he closes his eyes. "I'm yours, Hailey. No other woman even registers on my radar. You're it for me."

Parker leans back and it looks like he's debating something. I see desire in his eyes but also doubt. He stares at my lips, and I hope we're thinking the same thing because my body decides we're going for it.

I lean into him and press my lips on his. Parker doesn't hesitate. He kisses me back and sweeps his tongue over the seam of my lips. I open for him and he dives his tongue inside of my mouth, devouring me. I feel his hands roam my body – one goes to the back of my head to tilt my face more toward him as he controls this kiss, and the other goes to the small of my back, fusing us together. I moan at the contact and I swear I hear him growl.

I loop my arms around his neck and tangle my fingers in his gorgeous hair. He consumes me with his kiss, tangling his tongue in mine. He finally breaks the kiss, only to trail his lips over my jaw as he begins nipping and kissing the sensitive skin on my neck, down to my collarbone. Every single place he touches comes alive and I want more. The sting of his bites followed by the tender kisses has me on sensory overload.

Parker makes his way back up my neck where he nibbles my pulse point before licking away the sting. He pulls my earlobe between his teeth, which earns him another soft moan.

"Fuck, sunshine. You taste even better than I imagined."

He goes for my mouth again and we're caught up in each other's heat.

Parker pulls away and I lean forward, following him like a magnet. He chuckles and places a kiss on my forehead. "If I don't stop now, I'll have you naked and spread out on my desk within the next five minutes."

"Yes, please," I say before I can stop the words from falling out of my mouth.

He clenches his jaw and flares his nostrils. There's a fire in his eyes as he takes a breath and steps away from me, turning around to face the far window.

Shit. Way to ruin the moment with your big mouth, Hailey.

"I'm sorry, I shouldn't have—"

Parker is next to me in a second, wrapping me up in his arms.

"Don't apologize, sunshine. That was fucking hot. I want you. I want you so bad it hurts. But not like this. You deserve better than this for your first time." He trails his hands up and down my back. "You've been through a lot today. I'm not going to take advantage of you." He seems to say it to himself as much as me.

I nod and we break apart. He sits in his office chair and motions for me to come over. When I'm in front of him, he takes my hips in his hands and turns me before guiding me to sit on his lap.

I look over my shoulder at him and smile. "And this is helping cut the sexual tension, how, exactly?"

Parker laughs. "I don't know, but I can't stop touching you. I need you here while I make a few calls. Then I'll take you home."

Ice runs through my veins and I feel my muscles tense to the point of shaking.

Of course he's just going to drop you back off at home. What did you expect him to do? You refused to go to the hospital so what other choice does he have?

I feel his warmth surrounding me again, pulling me into his chest.

"No, baby, you're not going back with your dad. I'm taking you to my home. Our home. You're staying with me, okay? I won't let you go."

I nod into his chest, letting his light and warmth fill me up. I'm not sure what to say or think. I'm sure the rush of emotions and doubts will come later, but for now, all I can feel is safe. He continues to hold me close with one arm while reaching for his phone with the other.

"Hello, May? This is Parker, we met yesterday when I came in to woo Hailey?" He winks over at me and I roll my eyes. "Yes, the piece of man meat with a devilish grin." My eyes go wide and parker laughs as he repeats May's description of him. "I ran into Hailey on the train this morning. She's had a rough day..."

He looks over at me, gauging how much he can tell May. I nod my head. She knows better than anyone how my dad is. "She had a fight with her dad. She's okay now. I'm taking care of her." He pauses and listens to whatever May is saying. "I agree. She shouldn't come in for the next few days." I start to protest, but Parker quickly tilts the phone away from his face and kisses me before I can say anything.

He finishes the call with May by giving her his number and promising to take good care of me.

"I just have a few more calls to make so I can clear my schedule, okay, sunshine?" I nod, cuddling further into his warm chest. He smiles and kisses my forehead. "God, it feels so good to have you in my arms." I nod again, words still failing me at the moment.

He grins and continues making calls. I close my eyes, letting the smooth rumble of his voice blanket me as his hand on my hip slowly slips under my shirt, caressing the soft skin he finds there.

***

I wake up to Parker placing little kisses all over my face and stroking my hair.

"Hi, beautiful. You dozed off and I couldn't help myself. Are you ready to go?"

"Whenever you are," I say and smile up at him. He's so fucking gorgeous. Long lashes frame his sparkling blue eyes, and now that I know how his soft lips taste, I want more. As if reading my mind, he bends down captures my mouth in his. It's a short, sweet kiss.

"Then we better leave before I do anything else," he says with a wink as he helps me off his lap. I'm about to walk away when he catches my hips and pulls my back into his front. He gathers my hair and sweeps it over to one shoulder before bending down and placing soft kisses on the exposed skin. I close my eyes and turn my head to give him better access. When he gets to my ear, he says, "Thank you for trusting me, sunshine. Now, let me take you home."

I nod, and before I even open my eyes, he's leading me out of his office.

Chapter 7

I call my driver and we're on our way to my penthouse in under five minutes. In the car, I scoot Hailey closer to me, putting my hand on her thigh and rubbing small circles there to help soothe her. She leans into me and sighs. This feels like home.

I look over at my little sunshine and see she's wiped out. No fucking wonder. It's been a hellish morning for her, but she's taking it in stride. I got her to laugh and smile and even sleep a little while I held her in my lap. I'm sure she's partially still in shock and the flood of concerns will come later. I'll be ready.

The car stops in front of my building and I help Hailey out. Taking her by the hand, I guide her into the lobby, stopping when I feel my arm tug against hers. She's standing in the middle of the lobby, taking it all in with her huge green eyes. It's been a while since I've looked around the lobby. I guess it's kind of nice, though it's not what I pay a ridiculous amount of money for. That would be my penthouse.

I give her hand a small squeeze and she looks at me, a blush creeping over her face.

"Sorry," she stammers. "I feel underdressed," she says sheepishly. God, could she be any cuter?

I want to tell her that it doesn't matter what she wears because it'll be on the floor of my place soon enough, but that seems a little too forward. Instead, I lean in, brushing my lips against the shell of her ear, and say, "You're perfect just the way you are." She bites that damn lip again, making my cock stir.

We head over to the elevators and walk into my penthouse a few minutes later. I'm suddenly nervous about what she thinks. Is it too bare? Too plain? Too cold? Hailey lets go of my hand and wanders around. I follow her like a lost puppy. Her silence is killing me.

"What are you thinking about, sunshine? You know I can't stand it when you're quiet."

She turns to face me, her lips spread out into a breathtaking smile as she wraps her arms around my torso. I pull her closer, careful of her sore side.

"You might be the only one who thinks that, Parker." She buries her head in my chest and I stroke her hair, placing a kiss on top of her head. I hate everyone who made her feel annoying or like her voice didn't matter.

"It's true. I love your words. I love your thoughts. So tell me. What are you thinking about?"

Hailey lets out a huge breath and shrugs in my arms. "I guess I feel like I don't belong here. I mean this place is gorgeous and clean and I'm just going to come in with my dirty shoes and mess it all up. I feel like I should be wearing a ballgown or something," she lets out a little laugh at the thought.

I loosen her hold on me and kneel in front of her. She tilts her head down to look at me with a curious expression on her face. It's my fifth favorite look of hers.

"Sunshine, you belong here. I want you here. I want you in my life. Everything was cold and boring before I met you. I want you to make this your home, make messes, leave your shoes scattered on the floor, bake me all the Dutch letters. I want to trip over piles of your books and get lost in the sound of your voice as you tell me every thought that pops into your head. Can you do that for me?"

Her eyes glisten with unshed tears, but she nods and throws her arms around me. "Thank you," she sniffles.

"No, sunshine. Thank *you*. There was no light in my life before you."

I stand up and swing my arm under her legs, carrying her bridal style to the master bathroom.

"Let me run you a bath, you need to relax. It's been a hard morning."

She smiles. "That actually sounds kind of perfect. I can't remember the last time I lived somewhere with an actual bathtub." I start the water and add some lavender oil to the water. "You have bath oils?"

"I thought you might like them. I had my housekeeper pick some up yesterday."

"Oh." She blushes.

I walk back over to her while the tub fills up. "Hailey... can I look at your ribs?" She stiffens and instinctively holds her side. "You wouldn't let me take you to the hospital, but I need to see. Please, baby, let me see?" She doesn't move. "Do you trust me?" It's a bold move, but I have to know where we stand and how much work I have ahead of me.

"Yes." Her response is automatic, making my heart fucking soar in my chest.

I gently take her arms and unwrap them from her side. Peeling off her cardigan, I place soft kisses on her neck and shoulder. I kneel down in front of her and lift her t-shirt up. She makes one last-ditch effort to shield herself, but I catch her hand and place a kiss on her palm before guiding her arm to rest on my shoulder. I examine her porcelain skin and see a dark purple bruise already forming. Nothing looks broken, thank fuck.

I hate her dad for doing this to her, for hurting her, for all the other shit that lead up to this, even if I don't know the whole story yet. I kiss the very edge of the angry mark on her ribs and rest my forehead on her small tummy.

She runs her fingers through my hair and it's the best feeling in the world. "Are you okay?" She asks.

"Baby, shouldn't I be asking you that?" I look up into her green eyes. They do something to calm me. She's really here. She's safe now.

"I'm okay, Parker. I'm safe now," she whispers, ehoing my own thoughts back to me.

I nod and stand up, placing a kiss on her forehead. "Okay, beautiful. Take a bath and relax. I'll set some clothes out for you on the bed."

Hailey nods her head and murmurs her thanks. I want to gather her up in my arms and tell her she never has to thank me for taking care of her, but I have a feeling that would be too overwhelming for my sunshine. I'll have to be satisfied that she's here under my roof and under my protection.

***

Thirty minutes later, I've changed into sweatpants and a t-shirt and am sitting in my office, answering a few emails. I see my little sunshine wandering in wearing one of my t-shirts that hangs just above her knees and falls off one shoulder. I see she found a pair of my argyle dress socks that she has pulled halfway up her shins. She's too fucking cute.

"Um, hi," She says, suddenly unsure of herself. "I can go wait in the living room or something."

"No, come here, sunshine. I've been waiting for you. I can work later."

"Are you sure?"

"Absolutely. You will always come before work. I promise."

She beams at me and practically runs to my chair. Hailey surprises the fuck out of me by straddling me, making my dick is instantly hard. She threads her fingers in my hair and pulls me in for a kiss. I instantly melt for her, sinking into her sweet little body and letting my hands roam up her bare legs before slipping them under the shirt.

Oh fuck.

"You're not wearing anything under here?" I groan, getting harder by the second.

"Your boxers were too big so..." She shrugs. She has no idea what she's doing to me.

I growl and start kissing a line down her neck and then back up to her mouth where I pull her bottom lip between my teeth. I swallow her moan before diving back in for another kiss.

I should slow down, let her catch her breath and rest after the long morning she's had, but all bets are off once she starts grinding down on me. Jesus, I can feel the heat of her bare pussy rubbing against the thin material covering my cock. My hands slide up to her hips underneath the shirt, exposing more of her creamy skin. I help her find her rhythm as I continue drowning in her kiss.

I can tell the moment she rubs her clit on the soft fabric of my pants. She moans and jerks, throwing her head back. I attach my lips to her now exposed neck, nipping and kissing down the slender column.

"Are you wet for me, sunshine? Is that pretty pussy dripping for me?"

"Yes..." she moans as she continues to grind herself against me.

Fucking hell.

I want her so bad it hurts, but I know it won't be today. She's been through too much. I can give her want she wants though. What she needs. I reach down between us and slide a finger through her wet folds, circling her swollen, pulsing clit.

"Oh my God!" She moans.

"You like that, baby? Like when I touch you? When I play with your pussy?"

"Oh, fuck, yes, Parker..."

I pinch her little bundle of nerves and am rewarded with another moan. I kiss my way down to her perky breasts and cover one with my mouth, through the t-shirt. Another cry of ecstasy falls from her lips.

Sinking one finger into her tight little hole, I nearly come from how tight and wet she is. Hailey's whole body trembles as she lets out a shaky whimper. She feels fucking incredible. Her silk walls pulse around my finger as I curl it up to find her G-spot. At the same time, my thumb presses and rubs her clit.

"Fuck, Parker! Goddamnit don't stop! Don't stop!"

I love her cries, her dirty mouth. I suck on her left nipple through the shirt, pumping my finger in and out of her while applying steady pressure to her clit. I can tell all of the sensations are overwhelming her little body as she shakes all around me. I curl my finger and press on her clit while biting down on her nipple and she fucking explodes in my hands.

Hailey screams my name and throws her head back, squeezing her eyes shut, while her pussy clamps down on my finger again and again. I feel her juices pooling in my hand as her orgasm devastates her. It's the sexiest thing I've ever seen, knowing I put that look of pleasure on my woman's face, knowing I worked her body till she fell apart. I fucking come in my pants while she writhes on top of me, riding out the last of her pleasure.

My sunshine collapses in my arms, resting her sweaty forehead on my shoulder.

"Oh my *God*, Parker. That was...I mean, I've never...just...oh my God."

"Was that your first orgasm, baby?" She nods. *Fucking hell.* "You're so incredible, Hailey. So damn sexy. I love that I get to be all of your firsts."

She looks up at me and I take her mouth in a sweet and slow kiss before resting my forehead against hers. "Are you tired, sunshine? Maybe we should take a nap."

Right on cue, Hailey yawns and then blushes. "Yeah, I guess I'm kinda tired," she says with a sleepy smile. I can't help it; I kiss her one last time, then lift her up and carry her to our room.

Placing her on the bed, I go to the bathroom and clean myself up, throwing on a new pair of boxer briefs and some basketball shorts. Hailey gives me a questioning look when I return a few minutes later with a washcloth.

"It's to clean you up, beautiful."

She immediately rolls off the bed and stands up. "No, no, that's okay. Here, I can do it." She looks down at her feet and reaches her hand out for the washcloth.

"Look at me, Hailey." She glances up, her face red with embarrassment. "There is nothing to be embarrassed about. You're gorgeous, you come like a fucking goddess, and I want to take care of you. Let me clean you up and then we'll take a nap, okay?"

She doesn't move.

"Do you trust me, sunshine?" I know I've played that card already. It's partially so I can keep pointing out ways she does and can trust me, and partially so I can hear her say it. I love that she trusts me, I want more of it. All of it.

"Yes. I trust you, Parker."

"Good girl." I kneel in front of her, placing both her hands on my shoulders for stability. I begin wiping up the insides of her thighs, never taking my eyes off her. I move to her slit and wipe her clean. She trembles a little in my hands.

"Still a little sensitive, beautiful?"

She blushes and looks away. I toss the washcloth in the laundry bin and stand up, cradling her face in my hands. "Never be ashamed of your body, Hailey. I love that you're so sensitive, so responsive to my touch. I plan on worshiping every inch of you till I know your body better than you do." I place a chaste kiss on her lips and lead her back to the bed. Hailey crawls in one side and I follow right behind her.

"You'll stay with me?" she asks.

"There's no place else I want to be, sunshine. I told you I'm here for you."

She scoots over and rests her head on my chest, throwing an arm over my stomach. I wrap my arm around the small of her back, holding her close to me. My fingers slip under the hem of the shirt she's wearing, rubbing calming circles over her soft skin. This is perfect. She's perfect. I almost don't want to say anything, but I have to know.

"Can you tell me what happened this morning? Has he ever abused you before?"

"Not physically, no."

So emotionally and mentally. Fucking bastard. No wonder she has such low self-esteem.

"Why do you think things changed this morning?"

Hailey is quiet for a long time. Eventually, she lets out a breath I didn't even know she was holding.

"He wasn't always like this. I told you before he's kind of in between jobs. It's been that way for...a while. I was eleven when he had his first accident on the construction site. Mom had just died the year before, and he wasn't handling it well. He got workman's comp for a while, though that was hardly enough to cover the bills. Once the checks stopped showing up, my dad took on other jobs at factories or as a handyman, but he always ended up getting injured or let go from all of them."

"I'm so sorry," I murmur softly, kissing the top of her head.

"It wasn't all bad," she's quick to say. My woman doesn't have any clue what it means to truly be loved, and how bad she really had it growing up. "I hung out at the bakery all the time. My momma was good friends with May, so she stepped in and helped raise me. I think she knew things weren't good with my dad. She asked if I wanted to help her out around the shop even though I was fourteen. She paid me for my work, though all of it was unofficial, of course, until I was sixteen. By that time I was paying most of the bills."

"Jesus, sunshine. I'm so sorry," I say again, like a broken record.

"No, no that's not the point. Don't feel sorry for me."

She starts to push away from me, but I hold her tight.

"Baby, stop. I just meant that's a lot of pressure to put on someone so young. It wasn't your responsibility to take care of your dad. He was supposed to be the one to provide for you, to protect you. You're so strong and incredible for filling in that role, but you don't have to do it all alone anymore." I kiss her temple and guide her head back down to my chest. She snuggles back into me and continues.

"Anyway. He started taking out these small loans. At first, it was for a new chair and a new TV. I paid it off within a few months. Then it was a little more, to help tide us over until payday. I knew it was a bad idea, but dad felt like having the connections to get an off the books loan was a small safety net, I guess. I thought we were over it until I ran into Marcus the other day. Actually, it was right after I first met you on the train."

"Who is Marcus, sunshine?" I already don't like where this is going.

"He's one of the guys my dad borrows money from. It's not the first time he's found me. Usually, he'll just ask how my dad is doing. It's enough to let me know we owe a payment. But that day he was a little more aggressive."

I tense up. "What do you mean, aggressive? I swear to God if he—"

"It wasn't a big deal. He just grabbed me and told me my dad better pay up or he wouldn't like what happens next. It's okay. I'm okay." She places her delicate hand over my heart, calming me down.

"It's definitely *not* okay, but we can talk about that later."

She nods and takes a deep breath. "I came home that night and tried talking to my dad about the money. He was sober, thank God, so I actually got some answers."

"Does your dad drink a lot, sweetheart?" I slide my hand up her back and then run my fingers through her golden hair. Every part of her is stunning and I can't stop touching her.

"He didn't use to. Not until the last couple of years. But now it's almost every night." She seems lost in thought again, her delicate brow creasing.

"So, he owes money and he's a heavy drinker. Did you guys get in a fight about the money? Is that how..." I can't even finish the sentence before I tense up again at the thought of anyone hurting my precious sunshine. She rubs her hand back and forth over my heart again, soothing away my anger.

"Yeah. He was really drunk last night. I came home from the bakery and he wanted steaks for dinner. I opened my stupid mouth and told him we couldn't afford steaks when we owe one-hundre...a large sum of money to someone." I don't miss that she doesn't want to tell me how much he owes, but I let it slide for now. "But did I stop there? *Noooope.* I went and asked him if he was going to get a job. I just can't shut up."

"Look at me, Hailey." She does. "I need you to understand that none of this is your fault. I hate hearing you call yourself stupid or telling yourself to shut up. You are precious to me. All of your thoughts are precious. I know you don't believe it right now, but it starts with you thinking and talking better about yourself, okay?"

"Okay, Parker. I'll try."

I kiss her head again. "Good girl. Keep going. What happened after you asked him about work?"

"He pinned me to the wall and yelled. He didn't hit me, though. I made dinner and cleaned up, and then...we texted and called and you actually got me to smile."

She squeezes me and my heart just about burst knowing I helped her shitty night. Even though I wish she would have called me as soon as she knew he was drunk, I'm glad I brought some sort of happiness to her night.

"The next morning, I wanted to make breakfast for us, hopefully smooth things over, ya know?"

My girl is so sweet. I hate that she has been taken advantage of time and time again. I nod and encourage her to keep going. I know it's about to get ugly.

She takes a huge breath and exhales loudly, like she just wants to get it over with.

"When I took my dad's breakfast to his room, I saw him passed out on the bed. There were needles and drugs and lighters and I don't even know what else. I shook him awake and he threw me into the side table. I started thinking out loud about how we could fix it. Maybe if he knew I hadn't given up on him, he'd come back to me and be the dad I remember. I said I'd find a way to pay for rehab, and he...he...h-hit me," she whispers, shivering out a sob. "Everything in my mind went blank. I thought he was going to apologize, beg for my forgiveness. But he just said if he knew that's what it would take to shut me up, he would have done it years ago."

She's shaking in my arms, or maybe I'm the one shaking, there's so much anger flowing through my blood right now. How fucking dare he? Not only did he lay hands on his own daughter, on *my* sunshine, but he broke her spirit. He should have been nurturing her inquisitive mind and giving her the confidence to use her words. Instead, he made her feel annoying and stupid. I'm going to fucking kill him. But I have to take care of my sunshine first.

She's sobbing in my arms and I just hold her, stroking her back and telling her I'm here and she's safe. Eventually, Hailey's breath evens out and she's sleeping. Good. She needs it. I hold her close, unwilling to ever let her out of reach again.

Chapter 8

Hailey

I wake up tangled up in Parker. His leg is thrown over my thighs, his arms are wrapped around me, holding me close to his chest, and his chin is resting on top of my head. It's like he's trying to shield me from every bad thing, and I admit, I kind of love it.

I press a hand to his chest, marveling at the hard muscle underneath. The man must spend a lot of time at the gym. I kiss his chest and continue to feel my way down his torso, memorizing every muscle along the way. I make my way down to the hem of his shirt and slip my hand under, ghosting my fingers over his perfectly sculpted abs.

How can this Greek god of a man possibly find me attractive? I feel the muscles underneath my fingers flex and a low rumbling noise comes out of Parker's mouth.

"Hmm...you feel so good, sunshine. Love waking up to your touch." In a bold move, I run my hand lower, reaching for the growing bulge beneath his shorts. Parker's hand lightly grabs my wrist to stop my motion. "Don't start something you can't finish, sweetheart."

"Who says I can't finish?"

He's on me in a flash and before I know what's happening, he has me on my back, straddling me with my wrists held above my head.

"Fuck, Hailey. You're making it hard for me to control myself." He clenches his jaw and shuts his eyes. When he opens his eyes again, there's no denying the way he looks at me. It's a hungry look. "Jesus, seeing you laid out like this gets me so fucking hard. I have to have a taste, baby. You're like every one of my wet dreams come true."

He leans into me, but I stop him.

"Wait!" Parker freezes immediately and then backs off.

"Shit, sorry, sunshine, I got carried awa—"

"No, I want to keep going. But I want to see you first."

The fire returns to his eyes and he grins at me before reaching behind his back and pulling his shirt over his head.

Parker leans down again, this time placing his hands on either side of my head. I reach out and touch his shoulders, slowly dragging my hands down his chest, ribs, abs. I trace the tattoos I didn't expect to see covering half of his chest and down one bicep, ending just above his elbow.

"Do you like them?"

"Yeah...they're really fucking sexy," I say, continuing my exploration.

He chuckles. "*You're* really fucking sexy."

I slide my hands up his gorgeous body and around his neck, pulling him in for a kiss. Parker doesn't miss a beat. He consumes me in a desperate kiss and I get lost in the way his tongue wraps around mine before exploring every inch of my mouth. He swallows my moans before breaking the kiss and trailing his lips down my neck, nibbling on my pulse point.

Parker leans back and repositions himself between my legs. I instinctively jerk my hips forward, but he puts his hands on my hips to stop the motion.

"Not today, baby. Soon." I pout and he chuckles, leaning forward to bite my bottom lip. "I'll give you what you need, always."

Without another word, he leans back and lifts my shirt over my head. Parker takes my wrists in one hand and guides them over my head again.

"Keep these here for me."

I give him a questioning look. He smiles and leans down, brushing the shell of my ear with his nose sand lips. "Trust me, you'll like it." He nuzzles my neck and kisses a trail over my collarbone and in between my breasts. "Goddamn, sunshine. I could live right here, buried in your gorgeous tits."

He kisses his way over to my left breast and licks my nipple before sucking it into his mouth. He groans and releases my breast. Parker continues licking around my nipple and then bites the hard bud.

My back arches off the bed and I let out a sharp cry that turns into a moan.

He looks up and me from between my breasts. "Did you like that, baby?"

I nod, unable to form words.

He growls and holds my other breast in his palm, kneading and caressing my sensitive flesh. When he bites one nipple and pinches the other, I feel the jolt zip through my body all the way down to my clit. My hips jerk up, rubbing against his hard length.

Parker keeps his mouth on my skin, sucking, nipping, and kissing around my breasts while his right hand trails further down my body. I feel one finger slip into the folds of my wet pussy and drag from my wet hole up to my clit. I jerk and moan when his finger circles the sensitive ball of nerves.

"Fuck! Parker!"

"I love how responsive you are," he mumbles into my chest.

He kisses his way down my body. I tense up when I realize what he's doing. I try to close my legs. It's embarrassing to think of him staring at the most intimate part of me, let alone putting his *mouth* there.

"Uh-uh, baby, open up for me." He rubs gentle circles on my inner thighs, coaxing them open.

I shake my head, embarrassment heating my cheeks.

"Sunshine, what did I tell you? Never be ashamed of your body. I want to taste every part of you."

I hesitate, still feeling embarrassed.

"Do you want me to stop?"

"I-I don't think so."

"Are you scared or are you embarrassed? There's a difference, sweetheart. I'll never pressure you to do anything you don't want to do. You're always safe with me. I just want to make you feel good."

I nod, feeling the tension leave my body at his sweet words. I know he'd never hurt me.

As I spread my legs for him, Parker kisses a sensitive spot behind my knee, and then nibbles on my inner thigh before moving to my other leg and doing the same. He finally gets to my center and I'm shaking with nerves and excitement.

"Relax, baby. You're incredible. This pretty little pussy is soaked for me, isn't it?" I gasp when I feel his hot breath tease my soaking folds. "That's it, beautiful. I want you begging for my tongue."

He spreads my legs further apart and kisses the soft crease of skin where my legs meet my body. He runs his nose up and down both sides of my pussy, driving me crazy.

"P-please!"

Parker chuckles and I feel the sound vibrate through every part of me, down to my core. "Please, what, sunshine?" He uses his thumbs to spread my lips, still not touching me where I need him most.

"Please..."

He blows into my now exposed folds, the sensation overwhelming.

"Please lick me!" I moan, already on edge from his teasing.

"Gladly," Parker growls.

Parker's tongue dips into my entrance and roams up my slit till he gets to my clit. He sucks the nub into his mouth and I explode.

"Oh shit, oh shit..." I moan over and over.

Parker drinks up my honey like he's dying of thirst. He never lets up, bringing his thumb over my clit and massaging the sensitive nerves through my orgasm. He spears his tongue into my hole, in and out, and groans into my pussy, sending vibrations through my core, setting off another orgasm.

"God, Hailey. You're so fucking wet for me. I love tasting you, having your cum on my tongue. Do you like me eating out your greedy pussy?"

"*Yes...*" I moan.

He growls again and doubles his efforts, thrusting two fingers in my pussy while he sucks on my clit. I'm incoherent as I moan and thrash under his skilled fingers and tongue, grabbing his hair and pulling him closer to me, no longer able to keep my arms above my head.

I'm flooded with sensations, every nerve ending on fire. I feel myself gushing all over his hand and I can't bring myself to care. The tension builds in my core, my muscles tighten, preparing for the inevitable release. He bites my clit and I fucking lose it. I scream his name and come. *Hard.*

Parker licks me again, but I push him away, whimpering, too sensitized. He reluctantly pulls away, breathing heavily.

"Sorry, baby. You taste so good, I can't get enough of you." He crawls back up my shaking body, claiming my mouth in a soul-crushing kiss. I taste myself on him and it turns me on even more. Parker finally pulls away, both of us panting and sweating. He rolls onto his back and takes me with him, draping me over his body.

We both lay there in silence, getting our breathing under control.

"Parker..." I break the silence. "I... That was..." I don't even know what to say. Incredible? Life-changing?

"I know, sunshine. For me too."

"But you didn't even..."

"Doesn't matter. I could watch you come all damn day. I love giving you pleasure." I look up at him and bite my lip, unsure how to ask him for what I want. "What are you thinking about, beautiful? You know I want to hear everything inside of your head."

I blush and get the courage to speak. "Would you...do you want to shower with me? I'm kind of sweaty."

Parker jumps off the bed and scoops me up in his arms kissing me deeply as he makes his way toward the large bathroom. "You have the best ideas, my little sunshine."

Chapter 9

Parker

I set Hailey down and turn the shower on.

How did I get so fucking lucky?

My cock longs to sink inside of her, but I know it won't be today. Not yet. She's still too vulnerable.

I test the water and step inside, pulling Hailey with me. She loops her arms around my neck and pulls me in for a slow kiss. I pull back and kiss her on her forehead before turning her around and washing her soft curves. Hailey leans back into me, closing her eyes. Sweeping her hair to one side, I lean down and kiss her exposed neck.

"Mmmm...I love when you do that."

I rub my nose down her slender neck and lick my way back up before starting all over again.

She turns around with a mischievous grin. "My turn."

Hailey soaps me up, working her way from top to bottom. When the water washes away the suds, she kneels down in front of me, staring at my throbbing cock. Her eyes are huge and hungry as she looks up at me, practically begging me for permission.

"Fuck, sunshine. You don't have to do this." It takes every ounce of self-control not to shove my dick into her mouth and rut into her.

"Please, Parker? Show me how?"

Jesus fucking Christ.

I'm going to come right the fuck now if she's not careful. "Fuck, baby. Lick me, suck me, whatever you do will feel amazing." Her tongue darts out and she swirls it around the head of my cock. "Jesus," I growl as I throw my head back.

She places light, teasing kisses up and down the length of my cock. It tickles and feels fucking incredible. When my sexy little minx licks the underside of my dick from root to tip, I almost come.

"Open up, beautiful. I'm going to lose my damn mind if I don't get inside your mouth right now."

She parts her perfect lips and sucks me inside of her hot, wet mouth. Hailey bobs her head up and down my shaft, taking more of me each time. A low growl rumbles out of my throat at the sight of my dick disappearing in her mouth. She finds her rhythm, hollowing her cheeks, and sucking my soul right through my cock.

Hailey gasps and moans around my thickness, and I look down to see her hand between her thighs. She bucks her hips, getting herself off while she worships my cock.

"Fuck, Hailey. That's it. Play with that pussy for me like a good girl. I want you to come with me, baby. Come with me. Come right the fuck now!"

She trembles and moans around me, her orgasm sweeping through her tight little body. I roar my release, emptying rope after rope of hot cum into her mouth. I probably should have pulled out. I don't know how she feels about having my cum in her mouth, but I'm so fucking lost I didn't even think about it till it was too late.

Hailey whimpers and swallows everything I give her. Then the siren licks me clean. *Fucking hell.*

I pull her up and take her lips in mine, pouring out every feeling, every unspoken word, all of my pleasure and gratitude into this kiss.

"Goddamn, sunshine. You're incredible." I bury my face into the side of her neck and wrap my arms around her. My little sunshine. My precious Hailey. *Mine.*

After toweling off and getting dressed, I place Hailey on the bed and step out to order some food. Neither one of us has eaten all day and it's almost five. While I hate the circumstances that brought her here, I have to admit it's been the best day of my life.

I order about seven entrees and every appetizer they had. I don't know what Hailey's favorites are yet, but I will soon enough. While I wait for the food to get here, I go to my office and answer a few emails I've been putting off all day.

When the food finally gets here, I go looking for my sunshine. I hoped she would be relaxing and watching TV or reading a book. Instead, I find Hailey sitting cross-legged on the bed with her backpack, checkbook, notebook, phone, and a calculator spread out in front of her. She's bent over the notebook crossing something out and I can practically see the gears in her mind working in overtime. I knew reality would come crashing in for her, but I thought I could keep it at bay for a little bit longer.

"Hey, sunshine, what are you up to?"

She looks up at me with glassy eyes and a furrowed brow. I can feel the weight she carries on her shoulders and it guts me. If I knew she was in here anxiously spinning out of control, I would have ditched work in an instant to calm her fears.

"I don't know how this will work. Even if I work a ten-hour shift on Sundays at May's, I only have about three hundred to put toward the money we owe Marcus after paying rent. Dad said he needed at least five hundred for the next time I run into Marcus. Oh shit! I need to pay the electric bill too," she mutters while scribbling down another note. "I have to talk to my dad at some point. I just...Parker, I left him. Oh God, I *left* him. Is he hurt? What if he goes after May? He thinks I'm working today. He was so angry when I left, but..."

Before she can dig herself any deeper in unwarranted guilt and self-doubt, I crawl on the bed next to her. I pull her into my embrace, tucking her head into my chest while I hold her close. Hailey tries to break free, but I hold her against me, willing my strength and calm to wash over her.

"You don't understand!" she protests, trying to claw her way out of my arms. "I don't have anyone else! I don't have anything! I can't just skip out on work and bills and my own *father*. I don't want to be alone.

Please, Parker, I have to figure this out. Please..." She sobs into my chest, half-heartedly pounding her fists against me.

"Shh, baby. You're not alone. Stop fighting me, I'm here now. I've got you." I try to comfort her and cover her doubts with my love, with my faith in us, even if she doesn't see it yet.

"Yeah, but for how long? When will you get tired of me? When will you finally realize I'm no good? I'm exciting for now, your little tryst from the wrong side of the tracks, but soon you'll see what everyone else sees. I'm just an annoying little girl with no future. So please, put me out of my misery now, Parker. Let me go. Let me *GO!*"

She thrashes against me as sobs wrack her tiny body. My heart fucking breaks as she puts up all her walls and pushes me away. I'm not going anywhere. I rock her back and forth, riding out the storm swelling around her. Haily closes her fists around the fabric of my shirt, finally, *finally* pulling me closer instead of pushing me away.

She's shaking, and I can practically feel her fear and uncertainty seep out of her bones into my hands. I want to take it all away from her, make her believe in me, in us.

"Breathe, sunshine. I'm here. I'm not going anywhere, ever. Breathe for me, baby."

I feel her take a shuddering breath and let it out.

"Good girl. Again."

She takes another deep breath.

"That's it, sunshine. Again."

She pulls more air into her lungs as I stroke her back.

"Keep breathing, love."

Both of her hands are still gripping the fabric of my shirt. I cover her right hand with mine, forcing her to relax her grip. I move our hands over my heart and dip my head so it's resting on hers.

"Every beat of my heart is for you, sunshine. I will do whatever it takes to keep you safe, to take away your pain. All my money, my company, my home, my love...it's yours. I'm nothing without you, Hailey."

She curls her small frame further into me like she wants to disappear inside of me. I lean back and peel her off, but Hailey refuses to look up at me. I lift her chin up with my forefinger, but she squeezes her eyes shut.

"Look at me, sweetheart." She slowly opens her eyes, swollen and red from crying. "We will figure this out. You're not alone. Not ever. Do you understand?" My sunshine holds my gaze, searching my eyes for something. Finally, she nods, placing her forehead on mine. We stay like that for God knows how long, but Hailey's stomach growls, making us both laugh.

"Is my sunshine hungry?" I ask, smiling down at her.

"It would appear that several orgasms and a mental breakdown really work up an appetite," she says, grinning back at me.

"Well, then it's a good thing I got enough Chinese food for ten people."

After eating our weight in take-out, I tuck her into bed and wrap myself around her, nuzzling her neck and telling her how precious she is to me. I wait until I know she's asleep before succumbing to my own exhaustion.

Chapter 10

Hailey

Parker and I have spent the last three days in bed. Aside from eating, showering, and Parker answering a few emails, we've been wrapped up in each other's arms. We still haven't had sex yet, but we've done pretty much everything else.

It hasn't all been about getting each other off, though. We cuddle and talk and laugh. Parker likes when I lay across his chest with my head over his heart. He'll trace patterns all over my back and lull me to sleep. I like when he's sitting up against the headboard and I'm leaning against his chest, sitting between his legs. He'll wrap me up in his arms and kiss up and down my neck. But, honestly, as long as we're touching each other in some way, we both seem pretty happy.

I finally convinced Parker and May that I'm ready to go back to work. I wanted to go yesterday but Parker woke me up by burying his face in my thighs and licking me to orgasm. Twice. Then we showered together and I made him come in my mouth before he fingerfucked me into oblivion. By the time I came to my senses it was late to go into work.

This morning, however, I was ready. Parker insisted that I use his driver instead of the train or any public transportation. I fought him on it, but finally gave up. I've learned that Parker is relentless when it comes to my safety, and I must admit, it's kind of nice. Still, I don't want him to think I'm some delicate princess who doesn't know how to fend for herself. I have to put up a good fight every now and then.

***

May and I just got through the morning rush and we're cleaning up the aftermath.

"Sooooooo...." May says in an overly dramatic tone. "Tell me *everything* about Parker. And start with the important stuff. Is he as good in bed as he looks?"

"May! Stop it!" My cheeks flush red with embarrassment, but also with dirty thoughts of Parker. We might not have officially done the deed, but everything so far has been mind-blowing.

"Prude," she says with a smile. I scoff at her and laugh. "Fine, keep your secrets. Is he good to you, baby girl? Does he treat you well?"

"He's the best man I've ever known. He's attentive and protective and so kind. He actually *enjoys* talking to me. Can you believe that? He asks me what I think about things even when he knows I'm going to go on a rant."

May stops wiping down the display case and walks over to me, putting her hands on my shoulders.

"Hailey. I didn't know things were getting so bad with your dad." She looks at me with concern and regret.

"What? Where did that come from? I told you earlier, he's never done anything like he did earlier this week. There was nothing for you to pick up on, it just happened."

"Sweetie, things like that don't just happen. Physical abuse is always proceeded by emotional abuse, and from what I hear you say about yourself, it sounds like your dad was doing a number on your mind long before he laid a hand on you. And for that, I am sorry."

"May, it isn't—"

"I should have asked you about him more. I knew it was a sensitive topic since you never talked about him, but I thought I was doing a good job of looking after you while you were here."

"May, it's not your fau—"

"IT *IS*!" May all but yells as she throws her arms around me and squeezes me like I might disappear if she lets go. "I promised your mama I'd look after you. I failed her. I failed you. I should have taken you away. I'm so sorry. Can you forgive me?"

She releases me and looks at me with tears in her eyes.

"May. This isn't your fault. Parker says it's not mine either, and I'm working on believing him. There's nothing to forgive." I give her a quick hug. "You saved me by giving me this job, by providing for me when no one else did. I'll always love you, May."

She closes her eyes and nods her head, still gripping my hand tight. Finally, May takes a breath and looks at me.

"I promised myself I wouldn't get so emotional with you today, sweetie. But the thought of him..." she shakes her head in disgust. "Well, anyway. It's in the past now. And you have Parker. He's one of the good ones. He loves you, you know?"

"I don't know about that last part, but I know he's one of the good ones. He's the best."

"Mr. Man Meat might not have said them words to your face, but he sure as hell loves you. Trust me."

"Are you ever going to stop calling him Man Meat?"

"Probably not. I'm old and set in my ways." We laugh and get back to work.

May finishes wiping down tables while I gather up the garbage and take it out back. We joke about hiring someone to take out the garbage for us – I'm ridiculously short so it's difficult for me to hoist the heavy garbage bags over the lip of the dumpster, and May is a little too frail to make the attempt any more, though she'd never admit it.

I drag the two heavy garbage bags outside to the alley and set them on the ground in front of the dumpster to open the lid. As I struggle to lift the first bag up, I see a flash of silver and then feel cold metal pressed to the side of my head. Fear shoots through my body, prickling every nerve, and coating my skin in a thin layer of sweat.

"There you are," Marcus whispers into my ear. "Your daddy and I have been so worried about you."

"What have you done with him, Marcus?" I try to keep the panic out of my voice, which is about as easy as you'd think with a gun pointed at your head.

"He's the last person you should be worried about, honey. Didn't he tell you about his collateral for the loan?"

"N-no..."

He steps out in front of me with an evil grin on his face.

"You." I start to scream, but Marcus covers my mouth with his hand. I bite down causing him to curse. "You stupid, stupid bitch." He backhands me and I taste metal as my teeth dig into the side of my cheek. I spit out blood and regain some of my composure. There's obviously no way I could take Marcus down, but I could outrun him. I just have to get his gun out of his hands.

He wraps an arm around my neck and slams me against the brick wall. "I was told not to use more force than necessary, so as not to damage the property. If you have bruises and shit, we have to wait a few days till they heal before putting you on the streets. Looks like your daddy already fucked up your face a bit, so we'll have to wait anyway."

Marcus leans down so his face is inches away from mine. Feeling his breath on my skin makes me want to vomit.

"It's okay though, Hailey. I'll break you in while you heal. Then you'll work the streets and earn back what your daddy owes us."

I can hardly process his words before his mouth is on mine. Everything within me tenses and recoils at his touch. But then I realize I have an opportunity. While he's lost in his lust, his grip loosens on the gun. I feel his tongue slip in my mouth and knee him in the balls and bite down on his tongue. He releases me out of shock, and I hear the gun drop on the ground.

My brain is still catching up, but my body knows what to do. I put one foot in front of the other. Unfortunately, I run right into a behemoth of a man and fall backward, scraping my arm on the sharp edge of the dumpster. The behemoth looms over me, grinning like an idiot.

"She's got some fight in her, eh?" he grunts out.

I hear Marcus shuffle over to me, still recovering from the assault I gave his balls and tongue.

"Fucking cunt bit me." He spits out blood, right on my face. "You'll pay for that. I'll enjoy breaking you in, Hailey. I won't be gentle."

I see him raise the butt of the gun to my face and feel pain slicing through my temple before everything goes black.

Chapter 11

Parker

I hated seeing Hailey go off to work today. I know she loves her job, she loves May, and she wants to feel normal again, but something isn't right. I feel it. I know that sounds ridiculous, but I felt like I was going to lose her if I let her out of my penthouse.

However, after four days, I was running out of reasons to keep her locked up. And truth be told, I was falling behind at work. I agreed to let her go into the bakery today as long as she used my driver. I'll have to go visit her at lunch. I don't think I could stand to be apart from her any longer than that.

I've been texting her all morning because, yeah, I'm clingy and obsessive and I don't give a fuck. I know she has pastries to make and customers to serve so I don't expect her to reply instantly, but she's been doing a good job of replying when she has time.

The last text I sent was an hour ago though, and I'm getting worried. I know I'm paranoid. I know I'm overprotective and borderline crazy. Not borderline. Full-blown, head over heels, crazy for Hailey. And right now, I'm freaking the fuck out.

Me: Are you done with the morning rush yet, sunshine? I'd love to call you and hear your voice.

Me: Still busy? Text me when you get a chance.

Me: Sunshine, I'm worried about you, please say something.

Me: I should have stayed with you today I'm going crazy over here. Is everything okay?

I call the bakery and wait while the phone rings for way too long. Finally, May answers the phone. "I'm sorry, you'll have to call back later, I'm—"

"May, it's Parker."

"Oh thank God, Parker I need you to come to the bakery. Hailey took the garbage out and she never came back. We got busy and I didn't realize how long it had been and—"

I don't let her finish.

"I'm on my way."

I send one last text to Hailey and call for my driver.

Me: I'm coming for you, sunshine. Everything is going to be okay.

I practically jump out of the car before the driver even puts it in park. I run inside and find May pacing back and forth, gripping a rolling pin in both her hands as if she's going to brandish it as a weapon.

"Parker!" She throws the rolling pin across the floor with a surprising strength and runs up to me, arms out for a hug. "I'm so sorry, I'm so sorry, I never should have let her out of my sight!"

I hug May, and while I want to be mad at her, I can't. I know she feels like a piece of shit. I do too. It's my fault. I had a gut feeling and I still let her out of my sight.

"Shh, she'll be okay, May. I'm going to find her."

She steps back and resumes her pacing back and forth. "What can I do? I can't believe I let something happen to her again. I let her down again. *Again!*" May is muttering to herself at this point.

"May." My voice is strong and commanding. She stops and looks at me. "Stop. She wouldn't blame you, and neither do I. Stay here, lock up, and work on making us some lunch. I *will* be back with Hailey."

She nods. "Go get our girl."

I step out back and see two bags of garbage abandoned by the side of the dumpster. I see blood on the corner of the dumpster and more blood pooled on the ground below. Fear grips my heart and steals my breath.

I will motherfucking kill whoever hurt her. And I already have a pretty good idea of who took my sunshine. I whip out my phone and make some calls to have my people look up anything and everything about Marcus.

Stepping back inside, I give May a quick hug and head back to my driver. I need to make a call to my private investigator as well as get back up for when I find out where exactly Marcus took Hailey. Good thing in my line of work I've come across a few ex-military guys who are scary as fuck and don't need an excuse to crack some heads. It's time to cash in a few favors.

Chapter 12

Hailey

I wake up with a splitting headache. I try to sit up and realize I'm tied to a chair with duct tape over my mouth. I'm freezing cold and look down to see I'm only wearing a bra and underwear...and they aren't mine.

I feel the bile rise up in my throat to think that Marcus undressed me and saw me naked.

Oh, god, did he...

But no. I think I would feel different, sore, broken beyond repair. I feel terrified, but not violated. At least in that sense.

Thank fuck.

I take notice of my surroundings – I'm in a dirty, dank container. It's large and cold, made of metal. I'm guessing it's a shipping container?

Just then, the huge metal doors on one end swing open and Marcus steps through.

"Ah, my latest possession. So glad you're awake so we can play."

He closes the gap between us in three long strides.

I twist in the confines of my chair in an attempt to scoot away from the repulsive man in front of me.

"Now, now, little one. Let's not play hard to get. We're going to have such a good time together." He runs a finger from my cheek, down my neck, and between my breasts. "I must confess, when I made the deal with your dear old dad to have you work for me if he couldn't pay me back, I kind of hoped he wouldn't be able to come up with the money in time."

He grabs my breast and squeezes it roughly. I try not to scream; I don't want to give him the satisfaction. When he grabs the other one, however, I can't help the sound of shock and pain that comes out muffled against the duct tape.

"Do you like it rough, Hailey? Because that's how you're going to get it. Tell me, did your boyfriend take that cherry of yours, or did you save yourself for me?"

I close my eyes, trying to block out everything that he's saying and doing.

This cannot be happening.

Just this morning I was in Parker's bed. I was the happiest I've ever been. Why didn't I let him convince me to stay home?

Tears prick my eyes when I feel Marcus lick my neck. I feel disgusting. I want to burn off every part of my skin that he's touched.

He lets go of me and stands up.

Is that it? Was he just fucking with my head?

But then I hear it.

His metal zipper comes down, the sound bouncing off the metal walls. I close my eyes and whimper, thrashing around, doing anything to fight this.

This can't happen. I won't let it.

My eyes snap open when I hear a growl from the other side of the shipping container. A gunshot rings out in the small space, the shock tearing a shrill scream from my lips. The sound is deafening and all I hear is a high-pitched ringing in my ears.

It all happens so fast. Marcus' face twists up in rage and pain. He turns toward the doors before falling to the ground. Blood blossoms around his torso

My eyes squeeze shut. I can't stop screaming against the tape, shaking and thrashing, trying to use this opportunity to get away from whatever threat just took down Marcus. If I thought he was terrifying, whoever just shot him probably has even worse plans for me.

I feel the ties around my hands loosen and then come completely off. The piece of duct tape comes next. I still can't open my eyes.

Something warm is draped over me and strong arms lift me up. I open my eyes. I must be dreaming. I see Parker. *My Parker.* He saved me.

Chapter 13

Parker

When my contacts got back to me and told me about the full extent of Marcus' dealings, my stomach dropped. It was so much worse than I thought. Turns out sketchy loans were barely a blip on his radar. The big moneymaker was prostitution. It didn't take long to put two and two together. Hailey's dad couldn't pay the debt, so she would work it off.

Over my dead body.

I couldn't get to her fast enough.

Staring at Marcus' dead body does little to satisfy my rage. I wish I could string him up and beat him bloody. Rip out his nails one by one and then castrate him. But my number one priority was to get him the fuck away from my sunshine.

She's still in shock as I rush over to her and untie her hands and remove the tape from her mouth. I take my coat off and wrap it around her trembling, barely clothed body. I didn't miss that she was in a different bra and panty set than what she left the house in.

Motherfucker.

I scoop her up in my arms and kiss her forehead. When I lean back, Hailey opens her eyes and sears me with her pain and fear. My heart breaks in two at what that monster put her through.

"I've got you, sunshine. You're safe now. You're safe. I'm so sorry, love." I cradle her in my arms and kiss her nose and cheeks.

Hailey tries to speak, but nothing comes out. Instead, she grips my shirt in her hands and buries her face in my neck, like she's trying to disappear into me.

I carry her away from this nightmare and place her in the car, leaving her only to walk around to the other side and get in next to her. I instruct the driver to take us home before pulling her into my lap and gently rocking her back and forth. Hailey curls into me, still shaking. I rest my forehead on top of her head and whisper in her hair how precious she is to me, that we're going to get through this, and that I'm never leaving her.

***

When we arrive at home, I get out of the car, pulling her with me. I don't think I can let her go; I can't bear to be separated from her right now, maybe ever. I carry Hailey through the penthouse and into the master bathroom, setting her down on the counter while I run warm water for a bath.

She still hasn't made a single sound since I found her. I miss her voice, her words, her thoughts. Hailey just sits on the counter, wrapping her arms around herself and staring at me with wide, uncertain eyes.

"Let's get you in a bath. I'm going to undress you now, okay, sunshine?" I have no idea what's going on in her head. I don't want her to be afraid of me. She's been traumatized and it would be understandable if she didn't want me to touch her.

She nods her head and lets me take off the trashy lingerie Marcus put her in.

I scoop her up and gently place her in the water. Pouring soap on a washcloth, I wash Hailey off, inspecting the bruises and scrapes on her delicate skin. When she's clean, I stand up to take my clothes off and join her. I need to feel her skin on my skin.

When I step back, Hailey whimpers, her voice cracking. It breaks my heart all over again. She looks up at me, tears streaming down her face.

"I'm not going anywhere, sunshine. I'm coming in with you, okay?" She nods and scoots up in the tub, leaving room for me to come in behind her.

I pull her into my arms, wrapping her up in my embrace. Hailey curls into me, her face pressing against the warmth of my chest. I feel her nails digging into my arms as she tries to wrap them around her even tighter.

I fucking can't hold back the tears. I rest my forehead on top of her head and cry. My precious, beautiful sunshine is broken and hurting. I want to fix it; I want her light back. I want her voice and her laughter. I wish I could take all the darkness in her life away, make her pain my own so she would never have to feel it.

"I'm so sorry, Hailey. You're safe now. I'm here. I'm never leaving you again." I kiss the top of her head and hold her until the water grows cold.

I help her out of the tub and dry us off. She never takes her hand off of me. It's either gripping my hand or touching my shoulder, my back, my hip, anything to maintain contact. It guts me. She's like a scared little kid.

I put on basketball shorts and slip one of my t-shirts over her head. Scooping her up, I gently set her down in bed. I crawl in next to her and tuck her into my side. She's so small, so delicate.

I stroke Hailey's back and tell her over and over that she's safe and I'm never leaving. Her breathing finally evens out and she relaxes in my arms. Only when I know she's asleep do I close my eyes and join her.

Chapter 14

Hailey

I wake up in a cold sweat. Flashes of the previous day play through my head. I think I'm going to throw up at first, but I swallow down the lump in my throat. Parker has his arms wrapped around me, snoring softly.

I don't want to wake him when he looks so peaceful. I couldn't bring myself to speak yesterday. I didn't even know what to think, how to feel. He just held me. Parker seemed to need me as much as I needed him. When he climbed in the tub with me and cried, I tried to find words to comfort him. I hate that he's hurting because of me. Because of Marcus.

My stomach turns at the thought of Marcus. My skin feels dirty from his touch. I don't want Parker to touch me where Marcus touched me. I have to clean off Marcus. I have to get him off of my skin. Nothing else matters, just this compulsive need to wash the memories away.

I slip out of Parker's hold and sneak into the bathroom. Putting on the water as hot as it will go, I strip and step under the stream. The hot water stings at first, but I crave it.

I reach for a washcloth and pour soap onto it, raking it across my skin. Last night, Parker was so gentle with me, wiping away the dirt and blood from my skin. But right now, I need it gone. I need to scrub away Marcus' touch. I'm not sure if I'll ever feel clean again.

I rub the washcloth over my stomach, again and again. The skin is raw, but I keep going. It's not enough. I move up to my breasts, scrubbing between them viciously. Removing the top layer of skin still doesn't feel like enough. I know I'm going crazy by I can't stop. I'm disgusting. Vile.

The shower door opens, and I see Parker standing in front of me.

"There you are my little sun…" He stops and stares at me. I wonder if he can see the dirt and grease I feel all over my body. "Oh, baby, what are you doing?"

Parker looks hurt and worried. He places his warm hand over mine, stopping the scrubbing motion between my breasts.

"You're hurting yourself, love. Come here." He guides me toward him, but I jump back. I'm not clean yet and I don't want him to touch me when I still feel Marcus all over.

"It's not enough!" I squeak out. It's the first time I've spoken since yesterday and my voice comes out harsh and scratchy.

"What's not enough?"

"I'm still dirty. I feel it. I feel him. I have to keep scrubbing."

I know I sound crazy. Just call me lady Macbeth.

Out, out, damned spot! Out I say!

"Hailey…"

"No! I'm disgusting! I don't want you to see me like this," I stutter out before I start sobbing.

"You're clean, sweetheart. Don't hide from me." Parker reaches out for me again, but I jerk away, slipping on the wet tile and falling on the floor of the shower. "Hailey!" Parker kneels down and then wraps his arms around me, hauling me onto his lap. He still has his clothes on, but he doesn't seem to notice as the water pours down on both of us.

"You could never be disgusting, my love. You're beautiful and so strong. I'm never letting you go. Please don't hurt yourself, you are the most precious thing to me."

"But… but I have to get him off of me. I have to keep scrubbing him off of me."

"Sunshine, he's gone. He's never going to hurt you again, I promise. You can't hurt yourself without hurting me. You are everything to me, I can't lose you. I won't."

Parker rubs my back in soothing circles and nuzzles my shoulder before shutting off the shower.

"Come back to bed with me, sunshine. It's still early. You need to rest." I nod against his chest. The crazy thoughts seem to have passed for now.

Chapter 15

Parker

Hailey sleeps most of the day thanks to some Vicodin I had left over from a minor operation last year. When she wakes up, I'm right next to her, getting some work done on my laptop.

"Hi, sunshine. How are you feeling?" As soon as the words come out of my mouth I feel like an idiot. *How are you feeling?* What do I expect her to say? She feels violated, dirty, unworthy. God, I'm an asshole.

She stretches and lays her head on my arm. I adjust so I have my arm around her and pull her head into my chest.

"I'm better now that you're here," she says.

She's so fucking sweet, even after everything. I lean down and kiss her forehead.

Part of me needs to know what exactly happened with Marcus. I have to know what he did to her. Did he...*fuck*. I can't even finish the thought. My muscles tense. I know she's not ready to talk about anything yet, so I try to breathe and let it go. For now.

She senses my tension and places her hand over my heart like she's done before to calm me down. I rest my hand on hers and take a deep breath.

"He didn't..." I hear her whisper against my skin.

How could she know what I was thinking? I need to hear her say the words though.

"What's that, love?"

"He... You saved me before he could do anything.

I pull her onto my lap and she instantly curls up. A wave of relief passes over me as I begin to stroke her back. It's the only good news I've heard in two days.

"You don't have to talk about it, sunshine."

"No, I do. You deserve to know."

"You don't owe me anything, Hailey. I'm just happy to have you here in my arms." I give her a light squeeze to emphasize my point.

"Well, what if I want to tell you?"

"Of course, love. You can tell me anything."

She nods and proceeds to tell me how he got her, what he did and didn't do, and how grateful she is to me for saving her. Anger swirls around in my veins, but I remember that Marcus is dead and I have to be strong and calm for my sunshine.

"Thank you for telling me, sweetheart. I promise to protect you, always."

"I know," she says as she snuggles deeper into my chest.

"Are you hungry?"

Her stomach rumbles on cue and a small smile graces her lips. It lights up my world.

"Apparently so." She looks up at me with longing. Her eyes flicker to my lips and I know what she wants.

I have to be careful with her. She's so vulnerable right now. I lean in and brush my lips on hers, giving her a quick, chaste kiss.

She pouts a little, but then her stomach growls again and she hops off my lap.

Chapter 16

It's been a month since the incident with Marcus.

My physical wounds are pretty much all healed, even the areas of my skin that I scrubbed off. I feel stronger though. A little skittish, maybe, and I have had a few nightmares, but mostly I'm just so thankful that Parker saved me.

I've tried to show him my gratitude, but he refuses all of my advances. He'll cuddle me, hold me on his lap, and give me sweet kisses, but he doesn't seem interested in doing anything else.

The thing is though, I need him. I need him like I've never needed anyone or anything. I want to go back to before everything happened when we were enjoying exploring each other's bodies and discovering new ways to pleasure each other.

At first, I thought maybe he just didn't want to push me into anything, but I've made it *very* clear, on *many* occasions that I'm fine and I want him to touch me.

I woke him up the yesterday by stroking his gorgeous cock and kissing his neck. He put his hand over mine and guided it up to his mouth, where he placed a kiss on my knuckles.

Ouch. It wasn't an outright rejection, but it might as well have been.

I came to the conclusion this morning that he thinks I'm too broken to be with, but he feels guilty kicking me out. He probably feels responsible for me since he saved me.

But I can't live like this. It's too painful to have him this close to me, with him saying sweet things to me and providing for me but unable to really touch him the way I want to, to feel his touch like I need to.

I started looking for an apartment about an hour ago, when Parker went into his home office to get some work done. I'm elbow deep in research and making a pros and cons list of each apartment when Parker walks in.

"What are you doing?" His tone is clipped. I sit up on the edge of the bed.

Shit.

I didn't want him to find out like this. I was going to have everything worked out and ready to go before having the actual conversation with him.

"Uh...looking at apartments."

"Why?" he all but growls.

My heart is pounding against my ribcage and I swallow the lump in my throat. I try to collect my thoughts so I can present something at least remotely coherent.

"Because...because it's obvious you don't want me. And I get it. I'm damaged goods. You don't owe me anything, Parker. You're not responsible for me. You saved me, and now I can go on and live a good life or whatever."

Just saying the words pierces my heart. I don't want to leave him, but it's only going to cause me more pain to stay here and love him without being able to really be with him fully. *Love.* It's the first time I've thought that about him. I think I've always known it, but I've never put the actual word in my head. Now that it's there, it makes everything hurt so much worst.

I love him.

Parker is kneeling down in front of me, his hands on the outside of my thighs. He looks up at me with hurt and confusion in his eyes.

"What...how can..." he stutters out before taking a deep breath. "Why do you think I don't want you? I've never wanted anything more, sunshine. You're my everything."

"Really?" I say, a little too indignantly. "You could have fooled me!" I know I'm being a brat but goddamnit how the hell does he think I'd interpret his actions?

"Talk to me, love. What is going through your head right now? Let me in."

He's been calling me *love* lately but I don't know what it's supposed to mean. Now it hurts to hear him say it, knowing that I actually do love him.

"You won't touch me. You won't let me love you like I want to. I can't..." I choke on a sob, trying to keep the tears at bay. "I can't be here with you, sleep in the same bed with you if we can't be together In all the ways couples are together. But I understand you probably see a victim. I get it. I'm damaged. I..." No more words can make it through my sobs.

Parker looks like my confession caused him physical pain.

"Sunshine. I don't think you're damaged goods. Fuck, that's the last thing I could ever think about you. When I look at you, I see strength and resilience and brightness that can't be dimmed, despite life trying to put you out time and time again. I see beauty radiating from every part of you."

Now I'm the one confused.

"Then why? Why won't you even kiss me like you used to? I miss you. I miss you so fucking much. I need you, Parker."

"Hailey, I'm trying to give you space."

"Yeah, I noticed."

"No, listen to me, love," his voice is soft and sincere. "I want you. I want you so badly. This week has been torture. Lying next to you in bed every night without tasting you or feeling you or finally sinking into you completely, making you mine in every way... It's the hardest thing I've ever had to do. But I can be patient. I never want you to feel pressured or obligated. I know you've been through hell and I would never make you feel uncomfortable. I don't know how you're keeping it together, sunshine. I feel like I'm falling apart every time I think about that day." He takes a cleansing breath. "But I never meant to make you feel unloved. I'm so fucking sorry. Nothing could be further from the truth. I just don't want to rush you. I would never cause you pain. Not ever."

"Parker, I need you. All of you. I need to feel connected, normal. I trust you. Completely. Please...please touch me."

I take his hand and slide it up my thigh before placing it over my breast. He instinctively kneads the sensitive flesh and rubs his thumb against my nipple through the thin shirt I'm wearing.

He groans and leans into me, spreading my legs apart and nuzzling my neck. He nips at my pulse point and kisses away the sting. I feel his lips brush against the shell of my ear.

"Are you sure, sunshine?"

I nod.

"I need your words, love."

"I'm sure, Parker. Touch me, make love to me. I need you."

With that, he growls and devours my mouth. It's a wild kiss, full of passion and promise. He trails his lips over my jaw and down my neck, licking and sucking on my skin as he goes. His teeth rake across my collarbone and I moan.

"Fuck, Hailey. I've missed you so much. Your taste, your soft skin..." he rubs his nose down my chest.

Parker gently guides me to lay down on the bed, my legs still hanging off the edge. I feel him lift up my shirt, ghosting his fingers up my stomach, my ribs, my breasts. He lifts the shirt up and off, tossing it aside.

His eyes go to my naked breasts before I feel his mouth close around one nipple, licking and sucking. Parker moves to the other breast, giving it the same attention. Then, he trails kisses down my center, getting to the waistband of my pajama shorts. Hooking his fingers on the edge, Parker slowly pulls them down, along with my panties. He reveals my hip bones and sucks on each one before inching the material lower, lower, lower. I lift my bottom to help him remove them both completely.

I'm stretched out naked before him, while he's still fully clothed. He sits back on his heels, still kneeling before me.

"Jesus, fuck, sunshine. You're so beautiful. Perfect. You're perfection."

I feel his hands slide up my thighs pulling them apart, gently. He runs his nose up the inside of one leg and down the other. Parker leans forward and nuzzles his nose against my pussy before spreading me wide open and licking the sensitive skin where my legs meet my hips.

He lifts one leg over his shoulder and then the other. I feel his tongue parting my folds and licking my core. I jerk my hips and feel him chuckle against my pussy, sending vibrations to my very core. His hands slide under my ass and he pulls me closer to him like he can't get enough.

His tongue spears into my entrance, licking every inch of me. Slowly, so slowly, he flattens his tongue and drags it up my slit, finally lavishing attention to my aching clit. When he circles the tight bundle of nerves with his tongue I cry out.

"Parker! Fuck, that's it. *Fuuuuuuck…*"

He sucks the sensitive bud into his mouth and scrapes his teeth across it at the same time as he spears a finger into my tight hole. The sensations pull a moan from my lips and I arch my back off the mattress.

Parker curls his finger in my pussy as his tongue continues tracing patterns over my clit. Then he switches, darting his tongue in and out of my hole while rubbing my clit with his thumb.

"Oh, fuck, Parker, yes!"

He growls and it sends a jolt of pleasure throughout my body. He leans back, his eyes never leaving my pussy as he shoves two fingers into my entrance. Parker watches himself fingerfucking my pussy, and it's undeniably sexy.

"Goddamn, Hailey. Just…goddamn," he says before diving back in, licking and sucking the lips of my pussy before nipping at my clit again.

My orgasm rips through me and I fly up off the bed. The only thing keeping me in place is Parker's arm across my hips.

He never stops. Parker keeps thrusting his fingers in and out, reaching up and curling them into that special spot that drives me crazy. I feel another orgasm building quickly, and Parker doubles his efforts, fingerfucking me hard and fast.

"Oh shit, Parker, I'm..."

"Let go, sunshine. I've got you."

I explode again, gushing all over his hand. He removes his fingers and replaces them with his tongue, lapping up my juices and sucking me down.

He continues rubbing my clit with his thumb until it's almost too much. He's wringing out my pleasure as my body shakes and convulses at his touch.

"One more, love. Give me one more."

"I can't..." I pant, even as I rock my hips towards him.

He lowers his mouth back to my pussy, now dripping with my cum. Parker removes his fingers and places both hands on my hips, steadying me as he licks every part of my pussy. He alternates between soft and slow, hard and fast until I'm out of my mind. A third orgasm shoots fire through my veins and I scream out Parker's name.

"Good girl, that's it. Come all over my face, I fucking love tasting you."

I keep chanting his name, unable to remember any other words.

When the last of my pleasure drips out of me, I collapse on the bed, limp and spent.

"Fucking hell, Hailey. You come like a goddess," he growls, looking up at me from between my thighs. "So gorgeous. So fucking sexy. I'll never get enough of you."

I scoot up in the bed and spread my legs, urging him to join me. Parker stands up and strips down in record time before crawling up my body and nestling himself between my legs. Bracing himself over me with his hands on either side of my head, Parker bends down and kisses me soundly. Tasting myself on him gets me so fucking hot. He breaks the kiss and puts his weight on one hand, cupping my face with the other.

"Are you ready, love?"

"Yes," I answer immediately.

"Are you sure?"

"Yes, please, Parker. I want this. With you. I..." I trail off and turn my head.

Parker gently guides my face back toward his. "Eyes on me, sunshine. You what?"

"I...Parker, I love you."

He growls and takes my mouth in a demanding kiss. He sucks my tongue into his mouth and groans into me. "I've loved you since that first day on the train. I obsessed over you. I needed to make you mine."

"I'm yours."

He rests his forehead on mine. "And I'm yours, Hailey. Always. Forever. Never leaving."

My heart beats with pure joy as tears form in my eyes. How did I get so lucky to have this man in my life?

"Parker..."

"Yes, love?"

"Make me yours completely. I want to feel you inside of me. Please."

He groans and bites my bottom lip before kissing away the pain. "Anything you want. I'll give you all of me." He lines up his huge cock to my entrance and pushes a few inches inside. "Relax, sunshine. Let me into this perfect little pussy."

He kisses me, long and slow, as he pushes himself further inside. I whimper as he stretches me and fills every inch of me.

"Breathe, baby. It'll only hurt for a minute."

He dips his head to my neck and nips at the skin. I feel him tear through me, the pain spreading throughout my body. I grip his biceps, my nails biting into his skin. Parker swallows my cry and stays still, deep inside of me. Tears slide down the side of my face, but I keep breathing through the pain.

"I'm so sorry, love." His eyes are full of remorse as he kisses away my tears. "I promise it'll get better. Let me make this good for you, okay, sunshine?" I nod and he pulls back out, dragging his huge length along the walls of my pussy before pushing back in again. "Fuck, you feel incredible. You were made for me, only me. God*damn*, Hailey."

He gets a steady rhythm and soon the pain subsides, giving way to an incredible feeling of being full. Full of Parker. Finally connected to him in every way, as close as we can possibly be. I start to lift my hips with his, keeping up with his thrusts.

"Jesus Christ, you're incredible. Are you okay?"

"Yes..." It comes out more like a moan.

Parker grins and picks up the pace. Wrapping my arms around his neck, I pull him in for a kiss.

"More," I moan. He growls and sits back on his heels, throwing one of my legs over his shoulders. "Oh, fuck yes, Parker, fuck..."

The new angle takes him deeper, stretching me in the most delicious way. He brings his thumb down to my clit and begins rubbing circles around the sensitive ball of nerves. My legs start shaking and I know I'm close. I'm almost afraid of how big this orgasm is going to be.

"That's it, sunshine. I want to feel you come all over my big cock. I want to feel you squeeze me and milk the cum from my balls. Do you want that? Want me to fill you with my cum?"

I can only whimper at this point.

I thrust my hips up and take him deeper, chasing my pleasure and his. I feel something huge barreling through me, threatening to consume me completely. I'm right on the edge, the delicious tipping point. My muscles strain and tense to hold on to my last shred of control.

"Come for me, sunshine. Fucking come all over me. Come for me now!"

I scream, fucking *scream* as my pussy throbs and gushes and pulses pleasure like I've never known throughout my entire body. I come so hard I see white. I forget to breathe, completely enraptured by the sensations taking over my body.

"Fuck, baby, that's so hot, so fucking sexy. I'm coming, with you, love." I feel his cock grow impossibly bigger before shooting rope after rope of his hot, sticky cum inside of me. I feel it hit me deep, setting off another orgasm. "Christ, Hailey. Fucking incredible."

He's still rutting into me, prolonging our orgasms as we moan and thrust together as one.

Parker sets my leg back down on the bed and collapses on top of me, quickly rolling over and dragging me over his chest. We're both sweaty and panting.

"Are you okay, sunshine?"

"That was everything." I whisper.

He smiles down at me and wraps me in his arms. "*You* are everything, love. That was amazing. I can't believe I waited so long to do that." I laugh and hit him playfully in the chest. Parker leans down and captures my mouth in a sweet kiss. "I love you, sunshine. So fucking much."

"I love you too, Parker. So fucking much *more*."

"Oh, we'll see about that..."

He rolls off the bed with me in his arms and carries me to the shower where he proceeds to pull two more orgasms out of me. The sneaky bastard.

Chapter 17

Parker

The next six weeks fly by. I've watched Hailey blossom into a brighter, more confidant woman before my eyes. I hope I have something to do with it. I hate that I deprived her of the intimacy she craved for so long. My only goal was to make sure she felt safe with me, no matter what.

Hailey didn't have much of a choice but to officially move in with me after the incident. After I had my hired help dispose of the body, I called in a tip about the prostitution ring Marcus was involved with. I might have mentioned Hailey's dad as well. From what I hear, he's still on trial, but my sources say he will definitely be going to prison for a long time. Good.

My sunshine is too damn good for this world, and certainly too good for the hell her father put her through. I let him know that when I paid the motherfucker a visit before he was officially brought in on charges. I fucked up his face, broke his leg, and stomp-kicked him right in the lap. Serves him right. After getting involved with Marcus' dirty dealings and then selling his daughter to that monster, he doesn't deserve to use what is sure to be a tiny dick ever again.

After I wiped my hands clean of blood and made sure he was still breathing, I got to work packing up Hailey's hundreds of books. They are the only thing she wanted from her old life, and I can't blame her.

When I got home that night, my sunshine took one look at my bruised, scraped up knuckles, and she knew what I had done. Hailey didn't say anything, she simply led me to the bathroom and started stripping both of us down. She washed me up and then just held me. That was the moment our new life began.

Hailey continues to work at May's, though I convinced her to cut down from six days a week to three. She started online classes for a business degree, and I couldn't be prouder of her. My little sunshine is so fucking smart and motivated. It brings me infinite joy to watch her succeed.

She doesn't know it yet, but I'm planning on proposing to her tonight. We don't have to get married right away if she doesn't want to, but I want my ring on her finger. I want everyone to know she's mine. Since she's not pregnant yet, wearing a ring will have to do.

As an early wedding present for my new wife, I'm buying May's. I've been working with May these last few weeks to make sure she gets the most of this deal. She's old and wants to retire and she can't think of anyone else she'd want to take over for her. I know Hailey loves the bakery and I hope she wants to put the business degree she's working on to good use.

Yeah, I'm crazy. I want it all with the girl I met only two and a half months ago. And I'll be damned if I don't always get what I want.

***

Everything is set. I made reservations for one of my favorite restaurants in Manhattan and I rented out a train car on the 5. Yeah. Did you know if you have enough money, you can rent out public transportation? I guess most people who have that kind of money don't want to rent public transportation, but that's beside the point. It's perfect for Hailey and I. Our relationship started on the train, and I'd love nothing more than to see it move to the next level on the train.

I had the filthy thing scrubbed from top to bottom just a few hours ago. I'm not even charging the city for that; they can have it for free.

I told Hailey to meet me here at the station after work. She has no idea what's in store for her, but I hope it's a good surprise. She deserves everything, the whole damn world, and I get to be the one to give it to her.

I see my future wife coming down the steps and my breath catches in my throat. She's so beautiful. Even after all the shit she's been through, she's putting her life back together and reaching for her dreams – dreams she didn't even dare have a few short months ago.

Tonight, Hailey looks positively radiant. The sun shines through her golden hair as it bounces behind her. Those green eyes of hers sparkling as she sees me waiting for her. Her skin looks so soft and creamy, and when she smiles, I swear she's glowing.

She's wearing a blue cotton sundress that makes her look like an angel, and of course, she has on her converse shoes. I offered to buy her new ones in every available color, but she said she likes her old ones. Says they have character.

My sunshine walks up to me and I wrap her up in my arms, lifting her off the ground and taking her mouth in a passionate kiss.

We're both panting for air when we break apart.

"What was that for?" she asks. "I just saw you this morning and you're kissing me like we've been apart for years!"

"It felt like years to me," I smile as I set her down and take her hand. She smiles back up at me, but there's a hint of hesitation in her eyes. I almost miss it, but when it comes to Hailey, I'm aware of everything.

The train pulls up, and just like I planned, our car stops in front of us. There are ropes on the entrances, forcing people to walk down and find another car. I lead us right up to the ropes and one of the transit workers lifts it for us to enter.

"What's going on?" Hailey asks.

"Just wait, sunshine."

We step inside where the train car is decked out in string lights and sheer curtains, giving the space a soft warm glow. After I looked at her library, I curated a few hundred books that I she would like that she didn't have yet. All of them are currently stacked up on the seats, organized by genre and then author last name.

"Oh my god, Parker, what is all of this?"

I planned on taking my time, letting her look over the books, maybe make-out a little bit, but I'm finding it hard to breathe and I just want to know if she'll say yes.

Hailey is already walking ahead of me, flipping through one of the books. I step behind her and guide her to sit down on one of the few empty seats. Kneeling in front of my beautiful sunshine, I see she already has tears in her eyes. I hope they're happy tears, but I'm not so sure.

"Hailey, I—"

"No, wait, Parker." She chokes out a sob.

What the hell?

I can feel my heart ripping out of my chest. It hurts. So goddamn much.

Hailey puts one hand on my shoulder and uses her other hand to wipe tears out of her eyes.

"I have to tell you something first. I-I just want you to know before you do anything you'll regret. I didn't know how to tell you..." More tears roll down her beautiful cheeks.

"What is it, sunshine? There's nothing you could tell me that would ever make me love you any less. You know that, right?"

"Stop, just...don't say that yet."

Well, this is certainly not going the way that I thought it would. I take both of her hands in mine and kiss her knuckles before resting our hands in her lap.

"Tell me, love. You're killing me here. Are you okay?"

She nods and takes a deep breath.

"Parker, I'm so sorry. I wasn't thinking. We were so caught up in everything and...and I'm not sure how it happened. I mean, I know *how* it happened, obviously, but I-I didn't mean to trap you. I don't want you to feel stuck with me. I didn't mean for any of this, but I think you should know..."

"Baby, I love you. I'm so confused right now. Can you just tell me what happened?"

"I'm pregnant," she whispers. "And it's yours."

That last part has laughter rolling out of me. Of course, it's mine, I would never have any doubts. But then the first part finally catches up to me.

She's pregnant. With my kid. Our kid. Holy fuck. I'm going to be a daddy.

I look at her with all the love and joy I have exploding through my body. It guts me that she looks so scared. "Sunshine, I'm so fucking happy. I can't wait to be a dad and for you to be a mom." I kiss her belly again and again, picturing my kid growing there already.

"Yeah?" She looks at me tentatively.

"Yes. God, Hailey, I love you so much. I want this. I want us. You've made me the happiest man in the whole world. I'm going to be a dad!" I practically yell that last part. I just can't contain it.

"You're not upset?"

"What? No, sunshine, I'm the furthest thing from upset. I want you. I want our baby. I want forever, love. Does that sound good to you?"

She nods again, happy tears this time, I'm sure of it. I don't wait for her to change her mind. Grabbing her left hand, I slide the princess cut diamond ring on her finger. Hailey gasps and throws her arms around me. I stand up and turn us, so I'm sitting on the seat and she's straddling me.

"Yes, yes, yes, Parker! I want forever." She peppers my face with kisses, and I laugh as her lips tickle over my skin.

Hailey finally leans back to look at me and I take her face in my hands, placing a sweet kiss on her lips. She deepens the kiss and winds her fingers in my hair. My hands instinctively move to her hips and she starts grinding into me.

I break the kiss to rub my nose along her neck, nibbling her ear.

"I booked a spot at one of my favorite restaurants, but I don't know if I can wait that long to get you back home, in bed."

Hailey laughs and the sound goes straight to my dick.

"Well I'm eating for two now, so I shouldn't be skipping meals."

I sigh a very melodramatic sigh and turn her around so her back is to my front. It's less of a temptation this way. Still very much a temptation, just a little less so.

"Okay, sunshine. Dinner. Then you for dessert."

She nods and leans back on my chest, holding her left hand out in front of her, inspecting the ring.

"Do you like it?"

"Parker, it's incredible. So delicate and intricate. Thank you for knowing I wouldn't want a huge, gaudy thing. I love this. It's perfect." She turns her head to look at me and I can't help but kiss her again.

The public transit worker clears his throat. I had totally forgotten about him. He has no doubt had an interesting evening with us.

"I believe this is your stop, sir."

Chapter 18

Hailey

I know I told Parker I didn't want to skip a meal, but truthfully, I'm really horny. Like, *really* fucking horny. All the time. Apparently, that's the pregnancy hormones. But to be honest, it's also just Parker. He's so gorgeous and every time I'm with him I can't believe I'm lucky enough to have someone like him worship my body.

We get to the restaurant and place our orders. It's a lovely place, really, but I can't seem to think about anything other than getting Parker inside of me right the fuck now.

"Sunshine? Did you hear me?"

"Sorry, Parker. I, uh, I'm a little distracted."

His eyebrows knit together in worry. "What's wrong? How can I help?"

God, he's too good for me.

I lean over the table and he instinctively leans closer to me as well.

"What's wrong is that I can't stop thinking about what it would be like to have you fuck me in the bathroom here. You can help me by following me into the ladies room in about thirty seconds."

Without waiting for a response, I make my way to the back of the restaurant and go into the restroom. Luckily, it's a nice enough restaurant to have just one stall in the room. A few seconds later, the door opens and Parker's dark, hungry eyes roam over my body.

"I couldn't wait thirty seconds, love. I need you right fucking now."

He locks the door and storms over to me, grabbing my face and slamming his lips on mine. I feel his hands travel down the sides of my body, landing on my ass. He kneads the flesh there and pulls me into him so I feel his hard cock pulsing against me. I gasp at the contact and Parker takes the opportunity to kiss his way down my neck.

"Fuck, sunshine, when you said that at the table I almost came in my fucking pants." He continues to kiss my shoulder, pulling the strap of my dress to the side so he can bite me there. Parker spins me around and walks us toward the sink. We're both facing the mirror, looking into each other's eyes. "Put your hands in front of you on the counter, sunshine."

I do as he says.

He kisses my neck again, trailing his lips over the back of my shoulder and down my spine. Parker kneels behind me, and I feel his hands slide up my legs and thighs before grabbing my panties and pulling them down. He tucks the drenched piece of fabric into his pocket with a satisfied grunt.

Standing back up, I hear Parker's belt buckle and zipper, and then see him take out his massive dick, pumping it once, twice, three times. He places a hand between my shoulder blades and guides me down toward the counter. Then both of his hands grip my hips, pulling my ass up.

Parker flips my dress up to reveal my ass and bare pussy. He groans and lines himself up with my entrance. "Are you ready for this, sunshine?"

I moan and nod my head yes. He stares right at me as he slowly pushes his cock into my aching pussy.

"Yes…" I moan. "More, please, more."

He growls and thrusts himself completely inside of me. I push back against him as he begins rocking in and out of me.

"Jesus, Hailey, you feel so good. So goddamn tight."

Parker is hitting me so deep I feel like I'm going to come apart already. As if reading my mind, Parker pulls out.

"What? No!"

He smiles and stares at me in the mirror.

"I've got you, sunshine. You know I'll always take care of you."

Parker slides back into me, slowly, so fucking slowly. In and out, in and out. I feel every thick vein and ridge on his cock rub against the walls of my pussy.

Sliding his hand from my hip to my stomach, Parker caresses the skin there so softly. I look up in the mirror and his eyes are full of such warmth, thinking about our child growing there. Parker moves his hand lower, rubbing my clit with his finger while he picks up his speed behind me. I throw my head back and try not to cry out each time he rolls my clit between his fingers.

Parker bends over my body and cages me in, placing his hands next to mine on the counter. Our bodies fit together perfectly. I feel his abs tense and release as he bucks his hips into me, thrusting his dick deeper and deeper still.

"Fuck, Hailey, I feel you. You're so close. Come for me, beautiful."

I squeeze my pussy around his cock, earning me a grunt. He blurs his fingers over my clit and then pinches it, setting off my orgasm. I throw my head back in a silent scream, resting on Parker's shoulder. He turns his head to suck and lick my neck while my body pulses and convulses in his arms.

As I ride out the last of my orgasm, he grips my hips and slams into me again and again, pushing me higher and higher, his fingers resuming their sweet torture on my over-sensitized clit.

"Parker, Parker, shit…" I repeat over and over.

"That's it, love. Come for me again. I want to feel you squeeze my dick so hard. Come for me, Hailey."

"Come with me, Parker."

He groans and I feel his cock swell inside of me as the first wave of pleasure snaps my pussy around his thickness. At the same time, I feel him shoot his hot seed inside of me. We ride our orgasms together, throbbing and thrusting until we're sweaty and spent.

Parker places sweet kisses along my back and neck and then looks up at me in the mirror with a shit-eating grin on his face.

"I didn't know I was about to marry such a dirty, sweet girl."

"Who, me?" I ask with faux innocence.

Parker puts my dress back in place before tucking himself back in and zipping up his pants. He turns me around and lifts me up onto the counter, gripping my hips and positioning himself between my legs.

"Yes, sunshine, *you*." He captures my mouth in a sweet kiss that quickly turns passionate and then desperate.

I pull back, gasping for air.

"Careful, Parker. Any more of that and I'll need you to fuck me again before dinner is over. Who knows, maybe I'm an exhibitionist?" I quirk one eyebrow up.

Parker growls and attacks my neck with kisses and nibbles.

"How did I get so goddamn lucky to find you, sunshine?"

I can't answer. I'm too lost in his lips on my skin.

He kisses down my chest and between my breasts. Kneeling down in front of me, Parker places sweet kisses across my tummy before resting his forehead there. I run my fingers through his hair, massaging his scalp. I tug his hair so he looks up at me, unshed tears behind his eyes. "I love you, Parker," I whisper.

He stands up and wraps his arms around me, rocking me gently back and forth. "I love you so much, Hailey. You are so precious to me. You and the little life we created. How crazy is that?" he marvels.

"Not so crazy when you consider we haven't used protection even once," I tease.

Parker narrows his eyes at me playfully, then nips the side of my neck, making me giggle. "Love that sound, sweetheart. I want all of your laughter, every single day. You're all mine. My sunshine."

I nod into his chest and snuggle deeper into his embrace. I may be his sunshine, but Parker lights up my whole world.

Also by Cameron Hart

Check out my other popular series and books!

Mafia, MC, & Bodyguard Romance:
Moscatelli Crime Family Series[1]
Di Salvo Crime Family Series[2]
Chaos MC series[3]
Savage Ride[4]
Mountain Man Romance:
Men of Blackthorne Mountain Series[5]
Bear's Tooth Mountain Men Series[6]
Cowboy & Small Town Romance:
Roped in by Love Series[7]

---

1. https://books2read.com/u/mqBaze

2. https://books2read.com/u/m0odzW

3. https://books2read.com/u/bMVAOk

4. https://books2read.com/u/bMVlG7

5. https://books2read.com/u/3RYDvB

6. https://books2read.com/u/mVel7A

7. https://books2read.com/u/3RYlBY